THREE

Ann Quin

Introduced by Joshua Cohen

SHEFFIELD – LONDON – NEW YORK

This edition published in 2020 by And Other Stories
Sheffield – London – New York
www.andotherstories.org

9 8 7 6 5 4 3 2 1

This book is a work of fiction. Any resemblance to actual persons, living or dead, events or places is entirely coincidental.

ISBN: 9781911508847
eBook ISBN: 9781911508854

Proofreader: Sarah Terry; Offset by Tetragon, London; Cover Design: Ronaldo Alves after a Quin series design by Edward Bettison. Printed and bound by the CPI Group (UK) Ltd, Croydon, CR0 4YY.

A catalogue record for this book is available from the British Library.

And Other Stories gratefully acknowledge that our work is supported using public funding by Arts Council England.

Supported using public funding by
**ARTS COUNCIL
ENGLAND**

MIX
Paper from
responsible sources
FSC® C020471

INTRODUCTION

Three is the second of the four brilliant and enigma-ridden novels that Ann Quin published before drowning off the coast of Brighton in 1973 at the age of 37. The mysterious character S – the absent protagonist or anti-heroine-hypotenuse of this love-triangle tale – dies in similar fashion . . . or perhaps she's stabbed to death by a gang of nameless faceless men before her body washes up onshore . . . or perhaps the stabbed-dead-body that washes up onshore is someone else . . . It's difficult to tell. And the telling is difficult too. And I would submit that it's precisely these difficulties that make this gory story *normal*.

A British married couple, a dyad of faux-boho normies, provide the other two points of *Three's ménage*. Their names are Ruth (sometimes Ruthey, sometimes just R) and Leonard (sometimes Leon, sometimes just L). They take up with this young woman referred to only as S, who comes to share their summer-vacation cottage and their lives, her family-role ever-shifting from boarder-daughter to sister to lover.

The novel opens with the couple talking over the news of her recent death, in a conversation that flows unimpeded into the one-sided conversation of surveillance. S's most salient remains are her journals and sundry recordings, both audio and film, which document her relationships with and impressions of R and L, who greedily read and listen to and binge-watch these artifacts in the dark and dreary mourning-season that follows. In addition to these artifacts, whose contents seem constantly to rise toward narrative or plot, and then, like the tide, recede, R and L pore over their own diaries and compare their scribbled confessions with S's: S had an abortion, R and L are trying, or claim they're trying, to get pregnant; S had, or might have had, a drug habit; R and L prefer to lose themselves in drink, and so on; as this posthumous surveillance of S continues, R and L are themselves surveilled by stranger-neighbors, who are constantly poking their blossomed noses up against the glass.

Besides the fixed-state documents and recordings, the only constant in this world – in this over-upholstered world of inherited bric-a-brac, cats, goldfish, and tepid tasteless suppers – seems to be confinement itself and the lack of privacy it inculcates. All else continues to change in rapid currents: the news, the anxieties, the social codes . . .

2

Because this is such a frank and personal book, I will speak frankly and personally myself: Like Ann Quin, and like her characters, I too have had problems with monogamy and realism – those two fantasies, those twinned delusions, of How to Live and Reproduce Life (monogamy) and How to Represent Life and Reproduce its Representations (realism).

In *Three*, Quin tries to find solutions for these problems, or at least tries to dramatize the search for solutions, and it's notable that she goes about doing so in opposite ways: Through S, she *expands* her couple into a throuple, but does so in prose that insistently *contracts*, in a vicious condensation of third-person description, internal monologue, and 'interior' – house-bound – dialogue, none of which is isolated by conventional typography or punctuation. Instead of Victorian quotation marks or even Bloomsburyian dashes indicating speech, instead of paragraphing indicating shifts in point-of-view, here we have a jumble, all the modalities of the novel form set side by side like a hoarder's secondhand sitting-room furniture. R's speech, L's speech, R's writing, L's writing, S's firsthand documentation, Quin's own sham-omniscient accounts: all run into one another, verbiage bumping up against verbiage in a dim, narrow, junk-cluttered hall:

In the doorway he looked up, holding slippers and a book. What did you say? Boots—did you take them off before going in there? Yes yes. Still raining? Stopped. He went back into the room. She followed, picked up the cat placed his paws on her shoulders. How are your orchids? Not bad quite good really several almost seem to grow overnight but God knows what will happen to them while I'm away the boy's so hopeless. Well I warned you didn't I always the same you will take things on then regret the responsibility. That's hardly the point Ruth anyway I've been thinking we could really spend more time down here than we do. I don't mind the summer Leon but not the winter. Oh I don't know can be quite cosy with all the fires going and you're always saying how fed up you get with the parties and people in town. Yes I know but there are advantages I mean I have to see the specialist also I've been thinking of having an analyst. Oh not again Ruth we've tried all that and you know how bloody neurotic you get. But there's a good one really quite near too anyway we'll see.

The effect of this experiment, much like the effect of the open-relationship experiment, is to heighten the multiple claustral experiences on offer: the claustrophobia of monogamy, the claustrophobia of a cottage vacation; the stifling atmosphere of middle-class British domesticity that hasn't yet gotten into the swing of the '60s; the stifling atmosphere of 'the swinging '60s' itself, with its simultaneously entertained feelings of having gone too far, and of not having gone far enough; the literal hothouse where L grows his orchids; the cramped kitchens and bathrooms and beds where R spends so much of her existence cooking, cleaning, grooming, and sleeping or trying to sleep; essentially nurturing herself or a figment of happy, successful coupledom in lieu of being able to nurture a happy, successful birth-child.

Quin's 'reproduction' of her characters' artifacts represents perhaps her most daring attempt to break out of the straitening of both monogamy and realism. While the journal entries are presented in a fairly traditional manner – even poignantly traditional, with dates at top and discussions of weather – the non-written recordings, and the audio recordings in particular, are presented in a format that's more

poetry than prose, with the white space on the page made to represent silence or the hum of a tape reeling blank between utterances.

These interludes
which R. and L. listen to separately
and together
which they listen to separately-together
are based,
unlike the film recordings, which are contained by frames,
on the frameless voice 'itself',
on the rhythms of
the voice 'herself' even when him,
a voice cigarette-and-booze-weakened,
hoarsened even when whispering,
and like the voices of the radio, and the voices of the characters
reading the paper
aloud, they bring the news
the inner news as they break
with the breath and unspool into
sputter about, and I quote,
'Incidents dwelt on
imagination
dictates its own vocabulary.
Clarity
confusion.'

3

I don't want to overstay my welcome so as to third-wheel you and
this book, so I'll merely close with a brief comment on *Three*'s
number. Three was a fascination of Quin's: the number manifests
throughout her work; here, of course, but also in her novel *Passages*,
the stylistic heir to what you hold in your hands, and, even more
explicitly, in her fourth and final published novel *Tripticks*. Three
is the trinity of Quin's Catholic upbringing and the governing sum
of space (three dimensions) and time (past, present, future). Three
troubles the scales of dichotomous, guilt-and-innocence-judgment

and tips the dialectic. In classical psychoanalysis, we are told that our sex problems are always created through unhealthy binaries, either between ourselves and a mother, or between ourselves and a father, and never through the always healthier trinaries of other prospective sexual partners – people we might very much want to sleep with who might also very much want to sleep with us; people with whom we might not have affirmed our sole legal, ecclesiastical, and some would say patriarchal, fidelities.

Classical logic exists in the binary too and as such it describes mechanistic perfection. By contrast, trinary (also called ternary) logic describes the messiness of being human. In trinary logic, a statement can either be True or False or some indeterminate, or indeterminable, third value: ??? Quin's brief, bleak life coincided with the development of programmable or stored-memory computing, whose binary logic has since come to master our lives by lashing our pasts and futures together through the 1/0 digitization of all of our writings and recordings. In the '60s, trinary logic, which had no obvious computational or commercial applications, was primarily a mind game played by obscure academics who, tellingly, lacked a standard notation to express their fooling with triunity – as well as by Continental artists (Situationists) such as Guy Debord and Asger Jorn (do yourself a favor and google "triolectics").

The origins of trinary logic are to be found in Aristotle and his famous proposal – so apropos to a novel that devotes so much mind to beachside brutality – about a sea-battle that will or will not happen tomorrow: 'It is necessary for there to be or not be a sea-battle tomorrow; but it is not necessary for a sea-battle to take place tomorrow, nor for one not to take place—though it is necessary for one to take place or not to take place.' It's with this statement that Aristotle cast free will into doubt and introduced the problem of future contingents: how can we say that we know that something that has not yet happened, will happen? Future violence by the tideline cannot be true, it cannot be false, it can only be contingent, possible or probable. Quin's book is the acting-out of this conundrum on a more relatable stage: Our marriage will last forever; we will never sleep with other people; our sleeping with other people will never affect our marriage; we will always have all the sex we want; we will always want all the sex we have; S. will kill herself; S will be killed by others; we will cause S to kill herself; we will never believe, or admit to each other that we believe, that we were the cause.

In our over-recorded, interminably reproducible, and self-interested age, S becomes a martyr. For nowadays there is nothing more rare and valuable and even holy than the unknown, the unknowable, the third-way open and forever contingent.

Joshua Cohen, Tel Aviv, January 2020

For Bobbie and Bobb

A man fell to his death from a sixth-floor window of Peskett House,
an office-block in Sellway Square today.
He was a messenger employed by a soap manufacturing firm.

Ruth startled from the newspaper by Leonard framed in the doorway. Against the white-washed wall. A wicker arm-chair opposite
the Japanese table. Screen. Sliding doors. Rush matting. A mirror
extended the window. Gardens. A bronzed cockerel faced the house.

What's the latest then? Fellow thrown himself out of a window.
Ghastly way to choose. But Leon hers wasn't like that—I mean we
can't really be sure could so easily have been an accident the note
just a melodramatic touch. No one can be blamed Ruth we must
understand that least of all ourselves. Yes yes I know and one could
say it was predictable her sort of temperament. I don't know. You
mean you don't really care Leon? Ah you should know the answer
to that my love.

He shuffled a few shells, pebbles, covered his ears with two. Used
to wonder whether it was really the sound of the sea. I knew it
never could be. Ever practical Ruthey. We should have gone with
her Leon. She liked rowing out on her own. You went with her
sometimes. Only once or twice then felt I intruded. But didn't she
ask you to go the evening before? We had shopping to do. And it
was stormy in the morning even she remarked how the clouds were
low-lying mountains couldn't be seen either. She should never have
gone. How—how will we ever be certain Leon how? We're not to

blame remember that no one is responsible for another's actions—
any tea left by the way? A little left I've cut you a slice of lemon.
I'll have it without. Just as you like. She picked a shell up, turned it,
held up until the light shone through. She was happy with us Leon
at least at the beginning when coming to convalesce. Yes I'm sure
yes but when was that? Check your diary.

March 21st	Private View at Gallery Two
March 23rd	Dinner with the Blakewells
March 26th	S for supper
March 27th	Headache
March 28th	Same
March 29th	J phoned
March 30th	J's birthday

Your step-mother's birthday when we bought that expensive glass-
ware and she made such a face in fact I'm pretty sure she went back
and changed it Leon. Actually the day after when

March 31st	S moved in
April 3rd	R ill
April 4th	Lunch at the Club
April 5th	Petrinelli translation started

Was I ill at that time Leon? Yes your first abscess. Ah yes of course
I couldn't move my arm. Like a rotten onion. So you said yet I kept
it covered up. You were forever unpeeling the bloody plaster asking
how it looked. She was very patient. Sweet. After all she was re-
covering from her op looked after everything. Don't know what
we would have done without her really. Helped you too with that
book on Egyptian art or something. You mean Monolithic Mosaics
Ruth. Well anyway the one you both found so fascinating. Certainly her typing came in useful. Good cook too. Not bad none of
us ate very much at the time. She was on a diet though she hardly
needed to. Rather inclined on the plump side Leon you said so yourself I remember. Only when I first knew her but she changed perhaps the op and everything your black dress fitted her. Had to for
that party. Yes like skin. Far too short of course but she would have
it. Rings twisted half way round she edged one off, chafing the skin,
she looked at. You wouldn't drink anything at that do. You know

why. But you. . . . That's right but I wasn't usual false alarm. Yet you seemed pretty certain hadn't you missed one period? I never said that—never. Sorry thought you had. He cut two slices of lemon, poked them around in the cup. Oh hell let's have something stronger shall we? Don't think so. Mind if I do is there any ice left?

Hands motionless she gazed past the cockerel, marked a point between the trees, statues. The shadows of statues on the lawns stretched to the cliff edge. What shall we do Ruth it is our last day here fancy going out for a while? You're so restless. Just thought you might like a walk even if only round the garden down to the swimming-pool say or—or by the sea whatever you feel like? How can you suggest that? But the dead can't dominate like this besides she loved the sea you know that. Well I don't why do you think I went to all the bother of getting the pool? I wanted it too love. Yes Leon to have your theatre in during the winter. If I'd known you really loathed the sea that much I'd never have accepted father's offer of the place after all we could have easily bought a house further inland. Thought it something I'd get over conquer in time with you Leon—with the three of us here together. It's very calm today clear enough to see the rocks the river too might see salmon in the waterfall. You go yes go on why don't you you're dying to get out. It's not that. . . . Not what? He poured some more whisky out, breathed against the glass, flexed his wrist, until the ice clinked. Just something to do. Have you packed everything? Yes. I hope the car's all right we don't want another breakdown on the way back. She straightened cushions, placed objects in different positions, re-placed chairs, slid the doors apart, stood between, and faced the room. Aren't you going out then? What's the point? I thought you wanted to. Like a drink now? That's the third you've poured out Leon. All right Sherlock envious have one do you good relax for Godsake and sit down. I drank too much last night still quite headachey think I'll take one of my pills. Drink might do it love you haven't a migraine one have you? A little nothing to worry about. Where are your pills Ruth you know you should take them as soon as. . . . Upstairs be a pet and get them will you? Her head tilted to one side, she frowned, turned slowly round, slid the doors together, moved heavily towards the sofa. He banged the door. Sound of other doors banging. She moved swiftly to the table, picked up the glass, held for a time under her nose, she sipped, put it carefully back, and wiped a mark on the table. She rubbed a circle on the window, glanced out, stepped back, and collapsed on the sofa, hand hovered over eyes, face, her mouth moved, but no words came. He bent over, hair fell across part of his forehead. She stretched up and brushed it away. Here we are then do you want one or two? Just one I think thank you. He held the small white round tablet between two fingers while she took the glass of water, gulped several times, smiling she looked at him as he rose from a half-kneeling position. Like the curtains drawn? No—no just be near me sit here bring the chair up that's it oh darling could you pass me a cushion ah that's better much better. He watched her snuggle down, hair flattened against a blur of orange and black. Her hand held out, fingers nestled into his palm. How you feeling now? Not so bad. Just a minute get my drink. Pour me one. Really should you after the pill do you think so should you? Just a little one. No ice left. I'll have a piece of yours. Been in my mouth. Doesn't matter put it in. The lump slithered, fell across the table. Oh look what you've done Leon—polished that this morning too. Don't fuss not to worry I'll get a cloth.

She slipped the ice in, tilted the glass, and leaned over the sofa, watched a bird tap a snail along the path, against the terrace steps. There all gone now no trace left. Where's Bobo is he outside Leon? How should I know? Go and call him darling. You know he won't come if I call. Yes he will if you whistle go on be a dear will you? She fell back against the cushion, eyes closed. Won't you? He opened the french windows, looked beyond the terrace wall, the trees. Do close the door darling so cold. He stepped out, head craned forward. She watched him, his mouth pursed. Then his face away from her, shoulders curved. She shifted into a curled position. He went down the steps, treading on a snail, the remains he kicked against the wall. His head moved from side to side as he whistled. But stopped, head tucked in, shoulders hunched. He listened.

She stood by the window and tapped. He walked quickly across the lawn. Ran past the swimming-pool, the broken, unbroken, unfinished statues. The trees. Against the wind, spray that brought a wetness to his face. Eyes. He came to the cliff edge, panting, swayed at the top of the wooden steps that led to the beach. Two lines of gulls crying rose up. Amongst the tracings of gull marks, herons, other birds, a weaving line of footprints. He climbed down, stopped, head raised, his hand out. His collar up, he walked slowly back.

The cat perched on her shoulder, she pressed her face against the window. Rubbed her chin against the cat. Is it raining again? Seems like it. Bobo was in all the time—who was there? No one at least not by the time I got there bloody trespassers they know this place is private yet they still come. She moved around the room, the cat clinging, tail up. Still we don't get hordes like in the summer and by then well perhaps the Council will have done something. About time they did—where's my drink? Over there. By the way Ruth do you happen to know where that book is I'm reading? How should I know? They moved round each other. The cat swayed, his tail swung, sometimes touched her mouth, hair. She brought him down into her lap, pushed him into a lying position, held him there. Shall we have some music on Leon? If you like wish I knew where that blessed book is. Have you looked in the toilet? No. Bedroom? No. Well? He switched the radio on, twisted the knobs. Oh not so loud. How's the headache? Not so bad keep that ah that's nice wonder who's playing? Taking it far too fast second movement should be much slower. I like it turn up a little darling. Haven't we the record of this Ruth? Yes I think so. Well there's hardly any point. . . . Oh don't switch off darling such a beautiful piece yes wait this next bit I simply adore now listen to those violins isn't it heavenly? Much too fast. Wonder who's conducting listen listen isn't it fantastic of course the allegro's best she would have loved it. Doubt it. Yes she would. Hardly think so pretended she liked classical to please us. Not true Leon you know that's not at all true shhhhhhhh listen to the harp bit oh it's so pure—ah so pure. He sank into a chair in the corner, hummed and bent his fingers back. Wish you wouldn't do that ohhhhhh this bit listen isn't that cello good? Not bad. Wonder what orchestra shhhhhh listen now there can you hear that note bar repeated taken up by the violins? They're hardly in accord Ruth. What programme is it on? Some foreign station—that cat's smelling. Of course he isn't. Well something is. Probably your shoes. He carefully brought one leg up, crossed over the other, and inspected the sole. Ah the third movement is my favourite listen listen it's a live performance too hear them coughing? Another station. Are you sure? She bent over the radio. He gestured at the cat, who glared back, moved a little, hesitated, ears twitched. It is the cat. What was that? I said it's the cat that smells—smells to high heaven we should have got him doctored. Oh hell lost the station now Leon try and get it back. He fiddled the knobs. She rearranged some plants. One nearly touched the ceiling. Help me with this darling would look better in the corner don't you think? That's where she always said it ought to be. You disagreed Leon but I think she's right—I mean. . . . Just as you like.

They stood either side of the plant, leaves fanned out, rustled, as they shifted it. At least we helped her financially in the way of rent food and so on. Compensated for the family life she never knew. Adored you Ruth. I guess so. They lowered the plant, stood back, looked up to where larger leaves curved, spun into their own shadows. There's one thing I'm sure we made life a lot easier for her Leon. No doubt about that. I mean a home in town place of retreat here what more could a girl want? Wonder if she'd have made it on the stage if. . . . Who can tell there are so many girls dying to do the same. She certainly had talent those mime plays for instance. Oh those I must say I never had much time for them. You joined in readily enough Ruth. What could I do remain a passive outsider to all your games then? You seemed to enjoy them I rather thought. Well—well I'd hardly have thought you were aware whether I did or not. They looked at each other, quickly away, at their drinks. He drained his glass. She played with the rim, lips nudged the inside. She became transfixed by several men loading a cart in a field next to the garden. Stared past the statues, rhododendron bushes. I just hated those masks for some reason and you always chose the one I wanted anyway. But I never had the same one Ruth. And as for making the swimming-pool into that ridiculous sort of sunken theatre well really. . . . That was her idea. At the time you seemed to take all the credit always the same any innovation usually turned out to be hers or someone else's. That's a lie Ruth not true at all. Those ghastly statues of your father's too disembodied pieces of bronze stone and bits scraps of metal you tried making into flesh and blood participators or audience of your little charades frankly grotesque Leon quite quite horrible ugh. She elbow-leaned against the mantelpiece, looked in the mirror, smoothed her eyebrows, and began plucking them. He watched her hold the tweezers up, jabbing the air between the mirror and herself. Strange how she almost hypnotised you into believing things yes like a child like when you were ten years old no doubt except then you were a little smug king in your own right in your own little realm idealist always an idealist I suppose. We all have ideals surely when a girl. . . . Nothing oh nothing in comparison to your big ideas such as creating a new world imagine a boy of sixteen who thought he could do that. She powdered over the red tracks under her eyebrows, brushed the powder from her dress. What did you hope to prove by it all anyway? Prove Ruth—I just believed that's all saw myself as a sort of disciple. . . . An agent? If you like at least to begin with. Wonder what would have happened if it hadn't been for your step-mother's influence let's admit if it hadn't been for her. . . . O.k. but it was something while it lasted very real at least meaningful at the time though probably meaningless now yet it's the full measure of what I am. Ah yes you still have that fanaticism about you did you ever mention your role in the war to her? Indirectly after all one never knows how it will affect people besides she was hardly born when the war began and youngsters jump immediately to conclusions. You mean treason and all that? Well I. . . . Let's face it you were interned all those poems you wrote while in prison think of them all—all that stuff in trunks up in the attic we really ought to turn them out such a lot of unnecessary junk letters and things when we get back hers too. Never forget those weeks we should really have been shot Mother and myself no doubt would have been if it hadn't been for our connections. Two at least two cases full of odious love letters from some girl you professed you felt sorry for. Time measured by meals I concentrated on breathing remember that day in day out. I wouldn't have minded so much if you'd even gone to bed with the girl but not even that. Nights were the worst noises in other cells of other men I never saw. And those hysterical pleadings you believed her too that's what I found so incredible. When they came to let me out I was too weak even to lift my luggage. You're hardly strong nowadays always sleeping except of course when we go abroad then your stamina is extraordinary like when we were just married oh how well I remember those hot awful days trailing around museums and me nearly fainting with exhaustion but still you went on and on. The interrogation was merely a matter of red tape nothing more and afterwards ah then began that unforgettable journey quite quite unique what an experience. I longed to lie on the lido anywhere but no there was this church to see that palace to view paintings which must not be missed God how young how passive I was then allowing you to dominate me like that funny when I think about it now. She curled up in the wicker arm-chair, picking at the sides. By the window, eyes closed, he smiled. Then we passed over the border into the mountains fantastic quite fantastic the sun—faces of those from the south then the camp high up you know while on the way there that was perhaps the only time I was really terrified what the others might do say traitor treason on every man's lips quite expected they would ostracise me. Possibly done some good if they had Leon. Fortunately the place was full of refugees flotsam from all parts six months there amongst the mountains a free almost lazy time lying in the sun hearing the people from nearby villages sing dance in the streets sometimes we'd see their smiling faces bright eyes over the wire—walls—we threw messages across though they never answered only the girls did in their own way through their songs. How romantic you make it all sound. I was a youngster life was all there at least the other side and I was alive—alive Ruth. But suddenly it was over and poor little you had to face the big big wide world. You may well scorn but it was vital—necessary I don't regret a moment of it in a way I'd like to go back there some time. Back—back where? To those mountains hear that singing again. Well nothing is stopping you. Well maybe. . . . Still what's wrong with these mountains and the one we always mean to climb? Maybe next summer Ruth we'll have more time—when does the boy come as the plants in the summerhouse need a lot of looking after? That's the

8

trouble having to leave everything gets so neglected while we're in town. Such peasants here too can never trust them tell them to do something and when your back's turned have to watch while they do it and show them. Yes like beasts and how they stare too Leon have you noticed when we drive past that woman and her awful kids honestly given half the chance I think they'd quite happily see us dead? They're all right if you talk to them. But what on earth can one say they wouldn't understand just go on staring and once we're through the gateway I can hear them laugh. Well at least they don't muck about in the river and they're certainly not to blame for those nasty obscenities put on my notices. That awful vulgar crowd from the holiday camp they're the worst I do think the Council should do something about it. I ought to write them again. At least they should clear the rubbish away. Disgusting God knows what's there. I can't—daren't look. She used to though the countless dolls she brought back and tried restoring. As if we haven't enough junk. Mostly hers Ruth. Yours. Father's then. If you mean the statues well you know what I. . . . But what can we do with them no one will buy them the garden is the only place and besides I rather like a few of them lend something to the place a great pity they had to break up Hallucination Aphrodite father's favourite. Certainly not mine so grotesque didn't even have a head I mean was it a man or a woman that thing sticking out of what looked like breasts? He used the head Ruth for a later work. I think I prefer your own little efforts to any of his they are a whole and one can see what they are you haven't done any lately? No. Why not? Don't know haven't felt inspired perhaps. You should darling stop that nail-biting habit wish you wouldn't. What? What you're doing now makes them bleed does stain the sheets and everything besides it looks so ugly. He inspected a remaining strip of skin near the cuticle. She picked up her knitting, clicked the needles sharply together, pulled the wool away from the cat. Naughty Bobo you know you mustn't do that I think in a strange way he senses some- thing Leon perhaps even misses her seems so restless since. Very feline of course herself. Almost kittenish at times. I'd hardly say that. Oh yes love the way she prowled around curled up in chairs and those green eyes. Blue Leon she liked using my blue eye-shadow.

9

Certainly enhanced them. Put on too heavily I always thought. Knew what suited her gave you some good ideas Ruth terrific sense of colour those curtains in her room for instance I like the pattern geometrical shapes. Very her of course don't you like these Leon? Not bad purple is your colour. No violet darling thought they'd brighten this room up especially on dull days don't you think? They're all right. Well you helped me choose them. Think I'll go for a little walk. But Leon it's pouring. Soon clear. How I hated it when you both went off for those so-called long tramps nearly driven crazy here all alone Bobo at least kept me company. We didn't go out that often love. Then that horrid mist would inevitably creep over the whole place and I'd feel suffocated imagine you lost or fallen in a pot-hole until I heard you both laughing as you came up the path what did she talk about when you went out together? Nothing particularly. Nothing at all? Oh this and that—we always enjoyed the scenery. Scenery? Yes you know views birds flowers and things she seemed to know everything by its proper name. Made them up. How could she Ruth? I'm sure she knew nothing about nature not really. I remember she hated it if I picked flowers even the wild ones. You'd bring them back though all the same both of you covered in grass and leaves. And we'd find you frowning over a book or asleep and you'd pretend to be pleased. . . . I was of course delighted with your offerings but you know how certain flowers bring on an attack. He stacked his pipe, smoothed the tobacco slowly over. She put the knitting aside, stretched across the sofa, reached out, as if to touch something, someone, but fell back, intently rubbed the flowered covering. How's the head now? Still there are you going out does look rather miserable and it is getting dark Leon? Maybe for a little I want to see how those plants are doing next year who knows maybe we'll have something to show for our pains garden looks incredibly bare. Hardly seems worth doing anything darling when it all gets trampled on. Well I've plans to stop them bloody well will too get a high wall built all the way round that'll put an end to their vandalism. They'll still find a way over. Have cut glass on the top and wire yes that's it an electric wire soon cure them. And who's going to do that Leon who will you get to do that no one round here take years? We'll get the builders from town they'll do it. Draw the curtains please darling so murky out what's on the tele? Yes a really high wall with thick cut glass all the way round that'll teach them stop them from peering in too no privacy these days. He tugged at the curtains, straightened the folds, brought them closer together. Well think I'll just go and see my orchids. Put your boots on it'll be so wet out and don't forget to take them off in the porch when you come in. A high wall with glass on top is the answer then perhaps an electric wire running along just above the ground. Dinner's at seven so don't be too long darling I don't want to come and call you and do clear the snails from the path I so hate treading on them. She watched him leave, stared at the closed door, walls. Knitting, which she picked up, put down. Played with the cat without looking at him, sharply pulled her hand up where he had scratched, and pushed him away. She poured some whisky out which she gulped down. Became convulsed with a coughing fit, gripping her sides.

He stood in the archway of white. On one side the paint peeled in thin layers, ran into yellow crevices. He fondled a statue, the hands of heavy quarry stone, with his fists. Ran his finger down, between, up again. From one to another until he reached the summerhouse. Shutting the glass door carefully he leaned there, sighing, and looked round.

In front of the television she turned pages of a magazine. Her hand bound by a handkerchief. She slid her feet out of mules, brought them up, under a cushion. Looked now and then at the screen. Her mouth puckered, eyes red, which she rubbed. Cleaned her spectacles, breathed on slowly, held to the light. Reached for a cigarette, the pistol lighter, the metal shiny part she stroked, put down. She jumped up and opened the door. Switched on all the lights in every ground floor room. Opened all the doors, moved from room to room. Switched off all the lights, left the doors open, and crouched in front of the television. The cat curled at her feet, she caressed him with her toes.

A bee orchid leaned over from the moistness around, touched his mouth. The petals fluttered. He put the pot on another shelf. Touched others. Slits of brilliant colour amongst a mass of green dripping foliage. Roots emerged suddenly as he parted leaves. Thrust through. He poked about with his little finger. He murmured with pleasure, sometimes sighed. Leaves sprang back into place. Tips of red and purple dipped, shrivelled into the dampness. The darkness. He shone a torch upon those hanging above in open baskets, clusters of stumpy tuberous shoots. Still murmuring he reached up, brought one down, parted a layer of tiny leaves, and looked in. His fingers trembled. His body sloped. Face flushed in the one stream of light. He pressed the earth in, smoothed over. Paused longer at some, peered into centres, ran a finger along stems, pink against pink laid there. Turrets of intense purple. Wings. Tongues striped, tilted towards him. The light. His eyes darted from left to right. Movements that slipped between shadows. His shadow, broken in part by the glass, spread over the plants. He swung the torch round and smiled as arcs of light split the whole place into a solarium one moment, an ovolo of darkness the next. He switched the torch off, stood against a table, and watched the rain slide across the window. Breathing slowly, he listened with the plants that sucked, dripped around and above.

She went from room to room, closed windows, doors, cupboards. Tried on clothes, hats, shoes too narrow, hobbled to mirrors. Squeezed into dresses, struggled out, touched the material, traced the design. Folded, unfolded blouses, cardigans. Slipped them on, off, until the bed, floor were covered with layers of clothes. Into which she flung herself, motionless, face buried. She unfolded, opened an ornamental box, tried on jewellery. Bracelets slipped up her arms, she extended herself over the bed. Arms held up towards the light, her wrists twisted until the bracelets fell, jangled against each other. She put them on her ankles. Undid her dress, put a dozen necklaces on, some draped over her breasts. In front of the mirror she pulled her breasts up by holding several necklaces above her neck. The beads sprang apart, rolled at her feet, scattered over the carpet, under the bed. She crawled along, gathered them up, hands groped before her, either side, behind. She dropped the beads one by one into the box. Two remained, which she held against her nipples. Kneeling she looked down, swung herself from side to side. Her tongue slithered over lower lip, drew it in. She licked the beads, replaced them on the extended nipples, her head thrown back, knees parted pressed into the carpet, feet together.

He switched the torch on and off. Stared at the window steamed over. Leaves rustled against his head. He leaned farther towards until they separated. He rubbed the glass with his arm, hands. His face flattened against the door, he fumbled for the handle, and fell out. Flashed the torch up to the trees, down into a row of statues. Light revolved, rotated over pieces, parts of stone, bronze glistened, sunk into greyness. Oblong shapes, sticks of iron, metal rose from uneven ground levelled out towards the swimming-pool. He climbed down, torch held firmly, directed upon the rungs his feet edged onto. Reaching the bottom he looked at the square of sky, then down the slope to the platform covered by tarpaulin, which he pulled off. Climbing up he faced the way he had come. The torch held upright. Something scuttled behind, a flash of white dropped. Fell away. He watched the owl climb higher until the sides of the swimming-pool closed in.

She powdered her flushed face, neck, brushed her hair. Picked up the clothes and pushed them into the cupboard. She leaned out of the window. Leon is that you—Leon? A flash of light weaved into circles, moved closer, and for a moment fell full upon her face. She drew back. Listened to the steps on gravel. Sound of sea. Wind in the trees. The waterfall. Steps on concrete. Somewhere an owl hooted. She closed the window, pulled the curtains, and looked back at the room. The shoes scattered about. Pile of the carpet in places flattened. The eiderdown slipped over one side. She went out onto the landing. Did you take your boots off darling?

In the doorway he looked up, holding slippers and a book. What did you say? Boots—did you take them off before going in there? Yes yes. Still raining? Stopped. He went back into the room. She followed, picked up the cat placed his paws on her shoulders. How are your orchids? Not bad quite good really several almost seem to grow overnight but God knows what will happen to them while I'm away the boy's so hopeless. Well I warned you didn't I always the same you will take things on then regret the responsibility. That's hardly the point Ruth anyway I've been thinking we could really spend more time down here than we do. I don't mind the summer Leon but not the winter. Oh I don't know can be quite cosy with all the fires going and you're always saying how fed up you get with the parties and people in town. Yes I know but there are advantages I mean I have to see the specialist also I've been thinking of having an analyst. Oh not again Ruth we've tried all that and you know how bloody neurotic you get. But there's a good one really quite near too anyway we'll see.

He turned several pages of a book made some notes in the margins, adjusted his spectacles, squeezed, stroked his nose, and yawned. I've been thinking about her room too Leon though I know we don't really need the money but it would be nice to have someone there to help a bit and when you're off on one of your trips. . . . Yes yes of course we'll put an advert in. An older woman I think. Just as you like love though we'd be taking a risk with someone we didn't know at least we had known her for some time. I don't think that matters really depends on what paper we put the ad in. Are you sure you want to Ruth—I mean after. . . . It's the nights when you're not home I can't bear it all alone in the flat. But no one can get in what on earth frightens you? Didn't say I was frightened oh I don't know just a feeling. She brought her arms up, hugged herself. He shrugged, turned some more pages over. She went out into the kitchen.

The cat brushed against his legs, he pushed him away, picked the hairs off his trousers. Sound of saucepans, plates. He closed the door, stared at the cat on his chair, who stared back. Fucking thing go on get off get the hell out. He gestured, arms waving. The cat, ears pulled back lay flat, watched him move round the room, the chair. Fucking stinking animal she never liked you really either. He looked down, his upper lip curled. Yes there is something evil about you she always said there was. He bent over and hissed. The cat, back arched, sidled against the chair. What are you doing Leon poor Bobo what's he been doing then? She put the tray down, her hand out to the cat, who jumped off, and ran from the room. Oh look you've frightened him what were you up to Leon? Took my chair. Well it's not the only one darling and you know Bobo prefers that cushion.

They slid the sides of the table out, lit the candles in their glass containers. The flickering of the television, he watched, she fed titbits to the cat, who stretched and purred from the buffalo pouffe. Now and then Leonard burst into laughter, rocked himself backwards, forwards, held onto the table. More potatoes darling? Don't mind. Yes or no? She stood beside him, over him. He leaned back, twisted his neck. If there are some left thanks no no more that's plenty. How you can watch that programme just don't know I don't think it funny one bit. He pronged a potato, held halfway, and laughed until his eyes watered. She looked at the cat, made noises, clicked, sucked, her nose wriggled. Make the coffee Leon. When this is over ohhhhhhhhh ahhhhhhhhhh oh that's good. She picked the plates up, rattled them together, scraped the remains and put them down for the cat. Think I'll have an early night. What love? I'm going upstairs. Not a headache again? No just rather tired—if you want coffee. . . . Did you want some love? Doesn't matter. He pushed away from the table, and sank back. She shoved the sides of the table in. Don't forget we have an early start tomorrow. She paused in the doorway. Did you clear the snails away? Yes I guess so. But did you Leon they'll be all there in the morning and you know. . . . They'll be back again anyway especially if it rains in the night. Ah well goodnight and don't stay up too late switch the lights out won't you—come on Bobo bedbeds—be nice if you could wash up darling save us in the morning. O.k. o.k. She closed the door. He moved nearer the television, which he turned up.

She quickly slipped off her clothes. Pushed, prodded her face, peered at herself, lower lip protruded. She moved about the bedroom, picked up the shoes, dropped them into the cupboard. Clasping the transistor set she jerked round and round, held a corner of the nightdress, her head flung backwards, forwards until hair fell over her face. Across the bed on her back, she stared at the ceiling, curtains, door. Her fingers scratched the edge of the eiderdown. She switched the light out, and rolled over, hugging the transistor which she turned low, hand sliding up the aerial.

He watched the television until the commercials came on. Blowing the candles out, he sat before the desk, opened a book, but did not read. He opened a drawer, another, yet another, and tossed papers out. He sat hunched, surrounded by paper spilling over desk, the floor.

He went upstairs. Ruth have you seen my diary? She sat up quickly, shielded her eyes. Do you have to make so much noise you're so loud sometimes Leon? Have you seen my diary? You had it earlier today remember—do switch that light off. He came farther into the room, and looked round. Won't be here darling more likely to be downstairs somewhere have you washed up? Not yet I wonder where it can be—what's happened to this cupboard door then won't close good God Ruth all these clothes all hers? Yes and none of them really my size. What in the hell are we going to do with them? He pulled some dresses out, held them up. Charity I suppose. There's her tape recorder too. Journals—I think she kept a journal. Heavens I'd forgotten about that. Of course if she had a relative. . . . Just as well Leon I'm sure what she's put down or recorded can't be a pretty story. We'll have to play those tapes when we get back Ruth. A life there perhaps we'll find. . . . Oh do switch the light out darling my head. . . . Bad again eh? He moved towards the bed. She looked at him from under her arm. That's a new nightie haven't seen that one before? It was hers she never liked it anyway. Looks nice on you I must say. He pulled at the blankets and looked where the nightdress had crept above the triangle patch of dark hair, he placed his hand on. She brought her legs closer together. He watched her pull the blankets, sheet up, her face buried in the pillow. Ruthey. . . . Yes? Oh doesn't matter. He switched the light out, slowly undressed, pulled back the curtains, groped his way between furniture towards his bed. Lovely full moon. What was that? I said there's a full moon how's the head? Just tired so exhausted after everything oh darling can you draw the curtains a bit the moon's so bright. At the window he stared out. The statues gleamed, elongated shadows across the grass. A patch of water between the trees.

Buildings. Where lights are stars.
Hours become hands. Impressions stain. Spread. Recollections.
Angles caught in a mirror. Spaces between clouds
tide-marks. Never rubbed out
lying in
bubble-baths
under snow. Blowing faces. Hollows are eyes.
Shirts
clothes. On the line above. Theirs. Three toothbrushes.
Blowing bubbles. Glide over tiles
split
against windows
glass. The sea
sea.
Sun somewhere. Half-open doors. Glimpses gathered. Curtains
drawn back. An open window. Vase of flowers. A light.
Behind. But a face.
Woman naked
crushed
by grapes. Bunches. Breasts swing over.
Boy
thumbsucks.
Round off-white blinds.
Old man
hooked above lace curtains. Skyscrapers a meccano set.

Hoardings fortify. This flat reinforced concrete. Pterodactyl commemorated
spans
the sky. Slit of light. An eye secretes innumerable splinters. Breathe in moist
flesh.
Footsteps. Below.
Voices
threads. Caught in pavement cracks. Mouths. Theirs. She talks to the cat. He reads out loud. Speaks on the phone in his special voice.

His apparition
a white horse. Sun clasped. Blue lids wrinkled. Something discovered in rock crevices. Spirals of light. Across limbs separated. The delirium
delight of sea-lions crouched under pyramids. Architectural expressions barely formed. Landscape merged with space at night
clearer aspects. Of them both. Patterned
by water. Apprehensive
before reaching the shore
waterfall. Fish leap in line. Heard before seen. Somersault.
Birds
statuesque until disturbed. Wall-surround. Single dark shade across the river.
Ripple of a pond. Once enough. Breaking of ice under the surface.
Bats fall into
squashed figs. Clusters of dried fruit. Damp earth-covered leaves stir. Wings folded. Warm. Eyes. But bats are blind.
Humming wires. Each to each. A different hum. The wind.
Messages
from clouds
there.
Here faces. Lowered into a well. Fire escape straddles.

Anticipation
then. Sand integument. Grains blown into navel. Stone-studded
between toes. Laughter. Swallowed by waves
slow-moving
bodies chase white whales. Gulls. Hovered near. Not crying
that day
premonitions. Tips of wings
white
not so white. A phosphorus light followed them. From the water.
She called. He silent. Over rocks
silver-plated. Motionless.
Watch
listen. Inhabit the nights with a cardboard figure. Dangle from
waxed strings. A setting designed
for two. Their bodies
hands
fly round. Joined. Away. Back again. In an hour
cornered
by expectation. In the still air.
An ash tree
shakes.
A swallow settles. Mistaken for a garden monument. Surprised.
By their own movements
her eye
travels through light. His cannot avoid hesitation. A fly
end of summer-dazed. Bangs against things.
Panic. First day. Their furniture. Spaces measured.
Chair
desk
sofa
table
elongated windows. Lie down. Look up. Under-water. Birds in
flight
coincide with notes of music. Her fingers. Glide. Mouth curled.
A secret smile. Opening a letter in a crowded street.
Oblivious
reminiscent of a man crouched against a wall talking to his shadow.

Decisions. To put emotions as a pair of shoes under the bed.
Their bed
the dividing line. Wanting complete annihilation. At the highest
point. Incidents dwelt on
imagination
dictates its own vocabulary.
Clarity
confusion. Pursuit to the point of indiscretion. The moment one's
victim suspects. Evading begins.
Gleam in her eye. Forces the onlooker. Participator to turn away.
But aware of the
unexpected corners
creases. Around her mouth. He moves into private aquariums.
She peers through glass. Without her spectacles. Fingers knead
knitting needles. Clock-magnetic. Remarks on the weather
a pain
in her side. He crouched over typescript. Fingers snap.
Head jerks. Mistaken for a nervous tick. Cultivated. Mid-
conversation startles. Sidetracks
dismisses.
Wait
give
an aspect. They regard.

Surrounded by chairs. Animals released. Octopus faces gullet
corridor. Float from island to island. Inherited from both sides
Sofa. Flora-pregnated.
Chippendale chairs. Unchipped. Upholstered in blue.
They call turquoise.
Persian rugs. Second skins. For them.
Warm napkins
Silverware pawns. Salt-cellar dominates.
Rooms soundproofed.
Paintings

not hung
too small. Not small enough. But still-lifes she used to do.
Burglar-proofed.
China plates
on the wall. Glass doors. Concealed lighting. White curtains
transparent.
Nursery done in egg-shell blue. Empty.
A special place for the cat. Never used.
Visitors. Change of linen. Every other day.
Existence bound by habit. Hope. Theirs. Nothing to contend
with.
The worst effort not to contradict their next movement
At first.

A plan devised. For their amusement. With masks.
Situation
insoluble.
Three points A B and C on a rigid body in a straight line. When
the points A and C being given B is chosen such that the sum
of distances
AB and BC is as short as possible.
Suggestion A walks past B and C. A might turn. Stop. Shrug.
Walk on. B and C watch. Perhaps follow A. Or separate. Possibly disappear together. Variations endless.
Grimaces
behind
expressionless faces.
Gestures. Attempt communication. Worms cut in half. He
balletic. She stalks. Stiff. Thrusting the air around.
Sound of her bracelets only. He follows confronted by slits for
eyes. Dismay. Desipient. Absorbed. Interpreters in isolation.
Chameleons in company.
Shapes
construct their own fancies.

Reflections. A train window. Ploughed fields. Across
Pullman seats. Crows
stalk
their own shadows. He spreads. She huddled. While he sleeps.
Doors slide through a snow storm.
Petrified seascape
risen.

The hotel. A room. Three beds. Cupboards that never close.
Turn about. Green wallpaper. An old man bears hot chocolate
on a silver tray. They with the sheets up. He leers over.
Backs out. Round every corner
corridor. Wardrobe door flies open. Flash of mirrors.
Double exposure
repetitive. In semi-darkness she reclines. Pretends to read. He
over unknown desk. Doodles in margins. Too narrow for his
elaborate schemes. On narrow beds. Listening to the radio.
Coughs.
Croaks.
Manoeuvrings of someone next door. Going in the basin. She
heaves herself up. He stands over. Looks out of the window.
Retreat to the bathroom. For undressing. Connecting door.
Their whispers. She brushes hair. His. Childhood accounts
reconstructed.
First loves.
When they first met.
Rhythmically strokes her rings. Flashes of light. Divide the three
beds. One confronting the two pushed together
then.
Here. Light switched out. Theirs. A finger under the door.

Efforts to please
disregard
actions
reactions. His hand presses her knee. Fish caught in a pool. Early
evening alertness. She still sleepy.
Smooths out the sheets.
Skin
sand
ash. Sea that sinks away. Blue strips remain. Rocks tattooed.
With shells. Marks of creatures. Taut.
In suspense
wait
for the tide to turn. A rock rolled across the beach against the wind.
Laughter. Hers. The embodiment of something. Never quite
touched. Not heard at the time. He proud of his.
Applying a momentary power.
Impatiently.
Fibres
texture
of thought alone.
Travesty?
a little. Now.
Then.

Journeys down. By car. Roof off. Sky left surprisingly in one
piece. The sun a moon. From smog into mist.
Colonnade of trees.
Fall over ridges.
Trees
stacked in valleys.

Mountains
appear. Move forward. When one is static.
Retreat when approached.
Fold of hills. Held by shadows. Dead seas. Fortresses
of stone triads.
Armies
of cromlechs. Face east. Sound of hooves. Marching feet. Through
white flowers
swept
one way. Stones into sheep. Water endlessly stretches.
Gulls moan. Flap
cry across. But silent near. Around. The house.
Surrounded by trees. No sign of anything living. But bend closer.
Turn up stones.
Separate
plants.
Leaves.
Branches. These stir. Rotate. Forests stride in the night. Neglected
orchards. Where blossom deceives.
A composite of silhouettes in a yellow field.

There is a lake in the middle of the mountains. They say.

Midnight. Insomnia. Avoiding early morning
light. Shifts in an area. Outside
frenetic attempts. At reconciliation
here. The gardens
where men came. Lopped off branches. Those left. Stark.
Squat
no longer cut into clouds. Houses used to tunnel through.
Venetian blinds. Sky split by grass.

There
springing up. Statues revealed. His father's hobby.
Figures unfinished. Row upon row. Salute the house.
Arranged disorder.
Surround
the swimming pool. Some fallen. Broken. After storms.
Damaged
by trespassers. Pedestals remain. Watchtowers for the cat.
Embellishments
in their life. An attempt
to add
amend
defend. At first a preoccupied pose. An asset.
Observe
to be observed. Period of self-emasculation necessary. In the
beginning
moments hardly prepared for.
Mute
poised
by the waters' edge. Their bed. Running
their bath. Thoughts a gathering of threads. Attempt to put
through an eye of a needle. An hyperbola formed.
Gradually more and more cones fit together. But how innocent
are they.
How treacherous?

Their attention held
straying elsewhere.
Someone else.
Hypnotised by
a child
dogs
cats
plans to be put on an adoption society's priority list. Agnostic.

Fertility Clinics
injections
pills
specialists
psychiatrists
analysts
masseurs
osteopaths
palmists
clairvoyants
what the stars say
Interpretation of Dreams
Hypnotism
Yoga
Buddhism
The Way of Zen
Japanese art
Dead sea scrolls
Families living in one room
Reviews
Continental films
The Working Class
Profit and Shares columns
Turkish Baths
Hairdressers
Do It Yourself articles
Recipes for the Unexpected Guest
antiques
plants.   Provoking each other's choice.   Desires.   Worst fears.
Their voices cushioned by walls.
Before an open window.
In a doorway. Padding about their room.
Four walls.
There
a cracked mirror. Above.
The sky. Between green pillars. That do not over-reach.
Priestess

Prophetess
Clytemnestra. Parts readily adapted to. As mountains change
colour. By the season. Scrolls of parchment paper.
The mountain. Sometimes seen
that has to be climbed.
Pursued
by fantasies
fears
memory
by that other place.
The house
at the top
of the avenue. Four women. And the child. Old ladies
with paper bags
dressed in papal dresses. Hats. With feathers. Tinted hair. Colour
of rust. Streaked in the rain.
Auntie Marmee
she's so barmy
loved a soldier
who deserted the army.
Threatened with a knife
bribed by bread and butter. Puddings
her delight. Skirt to the ankles. A mouse ran up
into her corsets.
Her nephew idolised. His mother
paralysed. Overweight. Running for the bus. Grandma Alice.
Eau de cologne. Disinfectant. Mothballs. Lavender
her room
curtains drawn. Marmee Marmee where's my tea then? And
Marmee put aside her own cup. Slices of bread in the saucer.
She went rushing. Died in hospital
not knowing.
Auntie Polly. Kept to her room. Silver hair brush
crested
slowly
over herself. Carefully plaited. Unplaited. Reached for the purse.
Hanging from her waist. Black-velveted. Whispered at through

the keyhole
Auntie Polly Auntie Polly where's my dolly Polly?
She crouched in the middle. Of stained coverlet. Fingers
find
plait
purse. Marks of her dress. On the floor
Polly Polly put the kettle on. Her mouth parted. Over yellow
pieces of paper
letters. She wrote to herself. They said. Sound of the wind.
A north wind through the door. Growled under the mat.
Trembled the stair carpet. The doll's house. Handed down.
Covered in dust. On the landing. Trunkful
of clothes
Indian shawl.
Ostrich feather fan. Later found missing.
Gold and silver cones. Filled with treasures
discovered. Fallen from cardboard boxes. Beads from the bead
curtain. Unstrung. Divided kitchen from hall.
Exhausted from dancing to the wind. Under the back door.
Rolled
into corners
floorboards
mudpies. The dump. Round the back garden. It must be got
rid of
she said. Bending lower over the scythe. Grass up to her knees.
Forgetmenot eyes. Peered into seedpackets. But your father never
will. He nonchalantly nodding. All energy must be reserved for
the voice. They listened to records
at night
He jumped up
and pronged a note. Not quite a top C there. Not quite. You
can't go in now. Why not
why not? Because your father's practising so be a good child run
along and play outside. Through the window.
Picture of corpulent ancestor.
The landscape with cows.
Bookcase of classics. Dickens. Her favourite.

Medical ones. His. Convinced of some disease. While resting.
Glass cabinet
filled
with curios. Brought back from India. Her first. And only
marriage.
The grand piano. He confronted. Chest thrown out. Eyes
closed. Finger poised. Bowing. In bow tie. And tails.
The mirror
shook
with ovation. His foot tapped
Do Ray Me No Farcicality Do.
Arms outspread. Rigoletto. Aida. Tosca. Ideal companion
sought. At last. Sold the house. To buy her a ring. Pay for her
training in Vienna. Took on a nine to six job.
Testing soundtracks. Superannuation scheme. Guaranteed.
Gradual removal of belongings. Not belonging.
Men that came
took
the furniture away.
Piano
pictures
glass
chinaware
Indian miniatures. Including masks. While she was out working.
No time for games. Run along and play dear.
Presents
a Japanese fan. Pleaded for. Auctioneer's face scrutinised the
broken handle. I didn't mean you to keep it dear. We'll meet from
time to time then. On his lap. And if you ever get into trouble
don't forget you can always rely on your father of course.
Later
in a cafeteria. He had a thing about waiters. Safety in self-service.
There he is. Are you sure? She said. Don't turn round now he's
just behind. Watched in the mirror. Is she with him? By himself.
In a new suit. Still pepper tweed. Brown porkpie hat. Worn at
an angle. Handling the same pipe. Has he seen us do you think?
Has he

Breathless to her insistence. His calculated indifference.
A cup knocked over. Did he look up?
Meetings later arranged.
Walks in parks.
Waiting under clocks.
Walking
arm in arm. Playing up to the curiosity of others. Why do you
never call me Father then dear? Upper lip encrusted with sugar.
From a Bath bun. You want to go on the stage well why not.
Why not in the blood I suppose. Not on your mother's side of
course. Her father.
Hugh the Masher. Flaming hair. Flashing eye. Met at a village
dance. Her mother. Rosina. Disowned by the family. The
grandmother. Who kept bags of gold under the mattress. Whose
eyes in the portrait kept the children awake at night. Dreams disturbed by the Masher.
After closing time.
The moans
cries
of their mother. Died aged forty. On a Sunday. With all the
bells ringing. That's why I can't stand bells ever since. She'd say.
His tears the morning after. But he never drank in the summer
come Spring and the boats.
Later took to Meths. With old cronies. Met in the playground
shelter. Down by the docks. Younger sister made a round of the
chemists. Asking them not to serve him.
You never had a hand out like I did. Sister to daughter said.
What is there in life but to live it up. It's not a doctor she wants
but the police. That's what's needed. They shouted that right
there over her rolling body outside the pub.
Died
in her fifties. Elder sister not knowing why. And what happened
to John? The brother. Called the Prof.
Surrounded always by paper. Duck of the school. Scholarship
to the University. At the age of sixteen. Ran away.
Never heard of again. Strange family your mother's. He said.
Straightening his black tie. In mourning. For a dog.

If only she'd have made more of a scene when I said I was leaving you know begged me to remain well if she'd done that who knows I might have stayed been with you still. It was your mother's continual curtailing of my freedom that eventually made me decide. You will be home for tea I hope? Where have you been it's so late I've had the dinner on for you it will be stone cold or what a noise you're making cracking that egg. Things like that which

He scratched his eyebrows. Sighed. Lips drawn in. I must admit your father did have a rather mean mouth. One can always tell by the mouth I should have known better I suppose. She nodded. Prodded her own lower lip.

Caught in at the corners. But those years I wouldn't have missed for the world though it's hard to believe they were the happiest ever spent despite everything

yes in spite of

What did your father say to you then where did you go?

Well fancy taking you there honest you'd think he'd treat you to somewhere nice a good meal in a nice place at least considering he doesn't see you that often. What did he say when you met what was the first thing

That you have a nice speaking voice well I must say that's no thanks to him didn't contribute a penny not one penny towards your education. And what else?

If you ever get yourself into trouble for heaven's sake don't wait two months take a specimen of urine immediately.

Got a boyfriend yet still a virgin eh? Don't leave it too long well twenty-one seems rather old not to have these days dear doesn't it? Eyes crinkled

smudged underneath. Did he use mascara? Of course he dyes his hair how else could it still be so dark at his age? Second cousin's wife informed. Oh no I can't believe that I never saw him do it all the ten years

not once in all the ten years we. . . . Has he put on weight?

He was inclined that way. Funny can't imagine him as portly. Middle age spread how strange. The locket

searched for

with the photo
of him
in plus-fours. She in hat squashed to the eyes.
Arm in arm. The portrait of her at twenty-eight. Ah
even there she looks sad. Smiling. He sighed. Of course she
was never happy with him should never have married someone
twice her age just to get away from the family you know.
When are you seeing your father again? So sorry dear
can't possibly just impossible can't possibly see you tonight up to
my eyes in work. Oh that favourite expression of his up to my
eyes. She said. Closing the locket. Do you want this yes here
take the photo out if you like. We'll meet some other time dear
give me a tinkle at the office don't forget.
It is your birthday after all you'd think your father would send a
little something though of course he never was very good at remembering meant it at the time oh yes every intention you know
at the time. How much then five bob postal order ah well I suppose
that's better than nothing.
The day a card arrived
typed
sent from a firm dealing in hearing aids. Long time no see please
get in touch Your Affectionate Father.
Unsigned. Well what are you going to do? You ought to see
him dear really after all he is your own father and blood is thicker
than
Put into a drawer
taken out
hoarded
in handbag. Later mistaken for an appointment card. Put in
wastepaper basket.
The office. A building crammed into a corner of a main thorough-
fare. Pause in front of the dozen name plates.
Peer from the top of a bus. The escalator. In
restaurants
supermarkets
cinema
theatre. A pork pie hat. Teddy bear tweed. Suppose

Return to the house
at the top of the avenue. Name on the gate. Changed.
Now on hinges that no longer squeak. The outhouse gone.
A garage built. Balcony demolished. A high wall surround.
Roses cultivated. In place of wild flowers. Wall flowers
plants
in unbroken pots. Small bushes. Marshalled either side of the
path
uncracked. Crazy paving. Enormous plastic dwarfs. A gardener
mowed laid-out lawns.
Beyond the downs
a glimpse
of the sea. Dark glasses. Climbing down the hill. Hand slipped
through branches
a blueness
gathered. Slowly.
The dew pond
Devil conjured. Treading areas
proposed
by a god. Not dead. But bored. With eyes wide.
Calling the width
of ground
air. Between. Guarded by a perplexity given to extremeties. A
light held. In the spaces ignored. By a catalyst. Compared to
Forms split
yet measured. One
to the other.
A length
known. Here. Cross-sectioned. Separate
visions chosen.
In movements. From that other time. Senses reel upon themselves.

Avoid
the necessary disguise.
Yet not accepted in the pattern formulated.
So.
Hide atrocities. Shared. The end is the end. The beginning.
Now.
When omens swooped out of seamists. Encircled the tree.
Now possessed of an aerial. From regal sight
the others
watched. Returning from school. Their laughter. Satchel of stale
sandwiches. Tomatoes. Squashed in corners.
Crumbs
plasticine
crayons
coloured chalks.
Mittens. Stolen. Silver threepenny bits. She used for Christmas
puds. The ABC dish. Grey on white. But grey.
With stew from marrow bones. Potatoes left. In small yellow
lumps. Around the dish. That jumped over the moon.
Prunes
plums eaten only for the pleasure of Tinker Tailor
This year
Next year
Never. Never the right-sized gym tunic. The others wore.
Above the knees
stained. At least in uniform there can be no discrimination dear.
At the age
of sixteen. Cosmetic traces. Rubbed off on the bus
cloakroom
navy blue coats. Utility. Monday morning. Can Mother pay
half the school fees now the rest at end of term?
Face matching tie. Amongst the dark greys
browns of the convent. The sun evaded
chapel windows. Filtered. Over statues.
Saintly
faces
slyly accepted demoniac metamorphosis. And He opened the

bottomless pit and the smoke of the pit arose as the smoke of a
great furnace and the sun and the air were darkened with the
smoke of the pit.
Angels
Horses with two heads
Locusts. Hiding in the nuns' habits. Passing along
corridors. Doors. Sudden gaps in white walls. But black.
Rosaries
teeth clicked. At whispers
giggles. In corners. Playground laughter. Absorbed by their seal
bodies. Cloistered faces
cul-de-sacs. When questioned. Do they use face powder?
What can they wear in bed? Boarders had to wear shifts when
having a bath. The Reverend Mother. A monkey.
Long arms.
Black
folded.
Friday morning
inquisitions
punishment
penance.
A hundred lines. No games for you today. Austere Portias on the
platform
leaned over. Books of conduct closely studied. Above their bent
heads The Last Supper. Just cleaned. Baited breath at the list of
names. Alphabetically called.
Red knees
plaits
ringed armpits. Touching crosses. Exchanged for embraces
never dared pursue further. Beret pushed back. Into
satchel. Outside the gates.
Clandestine meetings with boys
from the college
A girl was seen kissing outside this school yesterday will she please
own up?
Red faces
those who had not dared. But danced. With each other.

During break. Close. Those who knew. Wanted to know.
Pictures of filmstars. In lockets. The one who taught English.
Eyes of a saint. Medieval.
In prayer. Her hands
across the blackboard. Gliding into regions. Never apprehended
at the time.
Her face
appears still. Must answer to. But never wholly acquiescent.
Ceremonial court. Of scarlet
gold.
Candlelight. Moths struggled. In the chalice.
Statues
moved. When the eyes half closed. Corpus Christi processions.
Wearing white. Petals thrown.
Kneeling
on hot tennis courts. Tarmac clinging. Hymns chanted.
Hell Mary full of grapes. Our Father who farts in Heaven.
Authority of those allowed to wear veils. Black in Retreat. Smuts
on smug foreheads. In honour of Ash Wednesday. The one who
had epileptic fits. Wanted to be Bernadette in end of term play.
Prayers delivered for a moment's release. From Irregular Verbs.
The Angelus. The lavatory. Refuge for comics. Pornography.
A love letter. Betrayal
crumpled
behind gym tunic. Navy blue knickers. My heart's darling. My
only love. Yours till death do us part. Worship of heroes. Fic-
tional. Search for parallels. Temporisers with fate. Transposed
from imagination. Restlessness. Uncertainty. Folding inside out.
Back again. Between creases.
There is repose. But now

Bodies separate finally. Acrobats. Whose horizontal bars have been
slowly sawn through.
Rituals. A room extends

slipping
held back
cling. Upsidedown. Reach up
over
under. Snake sheds its skin. In the mouth.
Eyes
ears
toes. Defenceless. Commanding. We'll pick up a whore.
A dozen boys. Ten-year-olds. You'll be theirs.
To do what they like with. Submissive to scenes of whipping.
But not the one she waited with. Black leather belt. I thought I
told you to be back at seven. Bend over.
Kneeling
on stained sheets
soft
wet
warm. The rain outside. A place.
Possessed. Be possessed. To possess. The coming. Into waves.
A shrunken moon. Between. Wet between
two moons. But back to back. The inevitability.
Mysterious stranger
brother
father
lover. Lovers.
Body composed of a series of revolving wheels.
Moves along faster than sound
through corridors. Endless doors open
close.
Sound of a train. Rattling over a bridge. Folds up in the terminus
of
the head
eyes. Signals.
Confirmed. Psychiatrists. Wouldn't you like to help a childless
couple then?
Eyes
slant eyes. Chinese serenity. Riveted on a silver propelling pencil.
You know there are dozens of girls who come to me and expect. . . .

Streets
elevators
houses. Pressed closer. A cab to a place near a park. Seven a.m.
Over-generous tip. Smiles. Knowing. Impression of a too
expensive hotel. Perhaps they didn't have a vacant bed.
After all.
Injected
made ready. In white. Like half drunk. Must not lose conscious-
ness. Various instruments. Wad of blood retained shape of
gynaecologist's finger. Low voices in an ante-room. Cylindrical
light above. Chromium. Breathe deeply. Push. Where is it—
was it big enough to see? Three months. What do they do with
it in a bottle throw away?
A cab back. Not enough change for a tip.

Dreams. Day dreams
fashioned
from white walls. His thoughts. Female semen seep through
undergrowth.
Lying in wait. For something. The unexpected. Disrupt
the certainties. He declares familiarity of the city. Knowing his
way
around
streets. One way. No entry.
Buses
Underground. Makes life more tolerable. After a party. Looking
out. On deserted roads. Untouched by the sun. She had retired
early. Believed herself pregnant. Then. Did the constructing.
Reconstruction begin? Build on what though
Experience
hope
habit. Theirs?
Almost accidental. An unconscious action at the time. Only
afterwards the predetermined appreciated. Alternatives given.

Manipulations they must never be aware of. The reshaping. As finely as her plucked eyebrows glisten still with water. His legs stemmed round furniture. They never hold hands. He marches ahead. They move round each other
wait
for the lift. He manages the gates. Their faces split by double bars. No longer smile. We won't be very late but don't wait up no don't bother really we
The noise of the lift. Their voices
remain.

Leonard leaned forward, legs apart, body suspended in an enclosed area. Two chairs. Table. Tape recorder. Ruth stared at her rings. Touched her hair. Of course being an only child makes a difference I'm sure. Strange she never talked about her father not even to you. Maybe we should get in touch with him Leon? Why should we after all it's surely up to him. Thank God I didn't have a father like that. But yours died when you were two Ruth so. . . . Yes yes I know still. . . . At least you retain an image I suppose. Quite honestly I never think about him. Is there any lemon left? Tea's cold you should have said. Doesn't matter. I can make some more. She touched the edge of the table. He fingered the spool of tape. Thought that a moth stain up there but it's damp Leon must see to it get this room redecorated new curtains furniture don't you think before we find someone else? Yes surely. He placed the spools carefully in the box, and struggled up, pressed against the table, loosened his tie. Perched on the table, legs swinging. Motionless, he watched her gather up the cat, who watched her mouth, eyes, while licking her fingers, tail quivered, back slightly raised. A window banged. Shadows of buildings opposite broke the room into a quadrangle. She whispered to the cat, face tilted nearer to him. What would I do without my Bobo my beautiful Bobo then? Leonard reached for his pipe, hesitated before the mirror. Wish you'd shave darling suppose somebody called. Are we expecting anyone love? No but you never know besides you look so awful. He stared into the mirror, fingers clasped, unclasped. Hell raining again. Close the window then. Beastly weather. Endless endless rain. Do you know Leon we hardly emerged towards the end while down there. She went out of course. Never minded what the weather was like. A strong girl. In some ways. Incredible the time she spent underwater. Almost amphibious. Liked going in with nothing on. You never do Ruth. Well one never knows who's watching frankly I don't know how she dared. Less inhibited. Oh I don't think it was that so much she was let's admit a bit of an exhibitionist. Only went in like that at night. Yes and how I worried I mean with all those nasty currents and you're not exactly a strong swimmer Leon if she'd been in danger. That day she should have known better. . . . But how can we be. . . . Everything seemed against us first the storm then the bloody car conking out like that. No storm here apparently. Swept the west even floods in some places. What day was it Ruth? The fourteenth wasn't it? No surely fifteenth. The fourteenth a Saturday market-day don't you remember?

October 14th Shopping with R bought new shirt and shoes. Storm on the way back. Car broke down. No sign of S.

October 15th Clear day. Sun at last. S hasn't returned.

October 16th Rain again. Still no sign of S. Informed police.

October 18th Boat found capsized. Coat identified. Also note in pocket—looks like suicide.

October 19th Two hours questioning by police sergeant. River and coastline dragged.

October 20th R in bed all day. Translation completed.

October 21st Dinner with the Blakeleys. A good hock.

October 22nd Orchids making progress especially Barbatum.

Could have sworn it was the fifteenth strange how one lapses over such things. We all know what your memory's like Leon. Hers remarkable. Unique. Devastating. Yet she never talked about her past not even to you Ruth what did you talk about—say when I was away? Nothing very much. How silent you were when I came

41

back quite embarrassing interrupting your little tête-à-têtes I nearly walked out again conspiracy yes that's what it was like. Leon what are these little black marks for I keep meaning to ask you here in the diary? Top secret. Oh don't be silly you don't keep secrets ever there's a black mark here there well? Can't you guess? Dentist appointments—no surely not so many? Far more personal. Oh no Leon really why in heaven's name how horrid putting things like that down. No more than your temperature chart love same thing in a way. Not at all it's rather nasty what you do besides mine's purely for medical reasons. And mine? He stood behind her, took the lobe of her ear between his teeth. Why on this day and that I don't remember oh darling not now we're being watched. What—who by? Across the way that nasty couple again they're always at it. Really? They watch spy on us the whole time. Then you must be watching too. She pushed him away, marched over to the window, arms folded, she stared out. Horrid people nothing better to do—remember that ghastly hotel Leon the awful wardrobe door kept swinging open as if someone were inside. Ahhhhhhh a ghost methinks that stalked the skeletons of our minds. None of your Shakesperian quotes please. It's not happens to be one of my very own. And that peculiar waiter who bobbed up from behind doors. The bathroom one that never closed properly. Had no lock. No keyhole. No hot water. And the audacity charging us that amount too. Those stags' heads in the hall. The parrot I'm sure was deaf as well as dumb. Food wasn't bad. Everything so cold. Admittedly the menu never varied. A meatpie face without the crust. What Leon? The waiter's. That's what she said afterwards. No wonder the place was empty. Gives me the creeps every time I think about it. She crossed her arms over herself, shivered, lower lip sucked in. She drew the curtains and stood back. I don't really like these you know Leon the design is too large must get the walls done up—those finger marks near the door and those above where the bed was look awful. Hadn't noticed myself. As large as anything Leon you know sometimes I think you're blind except for your blessed orchids. They faced each other across the table. She looked at the tape recorder, chairs, the walls. Why we came in here to listen I don't know. I'm going to have a bath do you want one? May as well. Run it darling will you? He whistled in the bathroom. Sound of water filled the whole place, gushed around, met water from other pipes, swirled, hummed above, below.

Against the wall she looked vacantly at her hands, legs. A ladder which she picked at until it shot up the length of her thigh. He appeared with a towel. Nearly ready love by the way what's for dindins—fish? Yes. Turbot? No haddock but Leon couldn't we go out I don't feel. . . . Well I did rather want to get on with the new translation we'll go out tomorrow o.k.? A triangle piece of light caught between the curtains at the top. She drew the curtains quickly together, faced the darker room and groped her way out.

Naked, bent over the bath, he manipulated the taps, threw in bath salts, toilet water. Steam wafted over the mirrors, window. There we are hot enough love? She nodded, stripped quickly, looked at herself in the large mirror above the bath. He splashed about, whistled, used sponge, back-scratcher, a large round yellow bar of soap. She knelt in the bath, adjusted her plastic flowered hat, arms slid down, hands slapped the water until it lapped over her belly. She wriggled about, explored herself with an oval bar of lilac soap. Yes we'll get those windows cleaned tomorrow and new curtains furniture even charge a bit more rent after all it's worth much more than what she paid don't you think so Leon? Just as you wish love entirely up to you. Get a good class of person I think. Be a sweetie and do my back will you? He swivelled round, planted his elbows on the sides of the bath. She leaned over. You're quite brown still. Gardening I suppose that hot spell wonder if those sun flowers will come up next year be nice if they'd grow several feet like trees? Soil isn't good enough Leon nothing will ever grow properly there. Not even that so much but those bloody trespassers can't be trusted trample on everything still we'll get that high wall fixed up. But what about the view darling I do like to see the sea? We can't have everything anyway the sea can hardly be seen from the house and it's not so far to walk if you want to. I know but still. . . . We've got to keep them out whole weekends wasted clearing up the mess they make. Why do

43

they do it? Boredom most likely a good sound whipping would teach them. You know something Leon I saw her dancing once with one of them on the beach I didn't mention it at the time. . . . Danced very well she had an innate sense of rhythm. I thought she looked obscene really the way her legs spread out and. . . . Well they all do that don't they? Can't see anything in it myself. The primitive urge Ruth quite natural really. Natural ugh when you danced with her I've never seen anything look so unnatural quite revolting especially at that party all our friends looking on what an exhibition don't know what they must have thought. They seemed to enjoy it certainly applauded even cheered. Out of politeness I saw their faces afterwards heard them whisper. Nonsense of course they loved it. Why did the Murpheys come to town then and invite the Blakeleys out to dinner and not us fancy ringing me up like that and saying they had such a nice dinner with the Blakeleys how could they? Well we won't invite them round again. But to think we gave them one of your father's little statuettes for their anniversary. Not one of his best it was a bit chipped. That's not the point Leon. O.k. that's lovely thanks shall I do you now? They reversed positions. She giggled as he brought the brush across her back. She leaned against the taps, breasts hung between, water slid slowly across the small blue veins. Her body shook, she watched her breasts slide against the metal surround. He squatted, passed the brush over, up, down. Ohhhhhhh ahhhhhhh that's lovely oh further up yes ah that's it. He edged nearer, teeth clenched. She shifted from side to side, her legs parted. Harder just a bit ohhhhhh ahhhhhh a bit lower yes that's it oh that's wonderful. He scratched at some pimples, inspected the flushed circles. Wish you'd keep still Ruth I can't do it properly ah that's better. Water's getting cold wait a mo I'll. . . . Oh darling don't bite like that oh no Leon not now noooooooh. He drew back, brush held against himself. They gazed at the purple flesh protruding from the water. You always have to get sexy in the bath Leon. Sorry. Well you must admit it's hardly the time or place. . . . I said I was sorry love. He watched the purple tip disappear, swallowed up by the grey water. She turned the taps full on until her body became more flushed in large patches, leaving a strip of plaster whiteness above the triangle of dark hair. She pushed her face under the cold water, arms flung out. He screwed his eyes up, scratched himself. Everything enveloped in thick steam. Water streamed across the mirrors, window. Arms stretched above her head, she placed herself next to the mirror, rubbed against it until a clear expanse appeared. His head fell forward, mouth open. She plucked at the plug, stepped onto the thick white matting, furiously wiped herself, whipped the towel round her back, legs, in between. He hauled himself up by the plug chain, peered into the mirror, pulled at the folds of skin under his eyes. Wonder what did happen to those masks Ruth did you look thoroughly through her things? No sign anywhere. Perhaps she took them with her. What would she do that for—I mean. . . . God knows. . . . Oh you've got my towel Leon yes you have look at the initials and do leave the bath the woman comes tomorrow. He rubbed vigorously at the lines of dirt. Never does it properly though. No use doing that it's always there. That woman isn't much good Ruth really can't we get somebody else time and time again I've pointed out that my desk must not be touched. It gets so dusty and if there's one thing. . . . Tell her to dust around the papers not put them in another place then. He surveyed the bath. She played with her hair, curled, flattened round her fingers. Much better when—well when she was around at least there was someone who knew how much these things matter. Such as reading your diary though of course that doesn't count. Did she well nothing very exciting or incriminating. What about those black marks do you think she knew what they signified Leon? Oh really what matter now? She sat on the edge of the bath, hands helped the water down. How many of them before we were married Leon how many? He laughed, tentatively touched himself with the towel. Dozens of course. Liar. In my dreams. Nasty wet ones which you still have. I don't. Sheets at least can't lie. Not as many then. I wouldn't know about that. He dressed, clipped on his already neatly tied tie, chin jutted out, frowning, he brushed his hair. Did you know she masturbated. Who? Yes she did told me one afternoon even suggested I do it. And? What a thing. What did she use? I don't know didn't enquire further. I thought most girls did at school

45

and so on. They certainly didn't where I went. Ah there well. . . .
He shrugged, threw the hair-brush onto the window sill. Wish
you wouldn't do that. What? Put it there and as you're ready
darling you could go and get Bobo's dinner poor thing he must feel
starved there are some fishheads in the bottom of the fridge only put
them under hot water he doesn't like them cold and don't give him
more than two he sicks it up all over the place. Time that animal
was put to sleep. Oh darling how can you say that poor Bobo he's
part of the family now I'd die simply die if he went. Beginning to
smell too and why you never trained him properly to his earth
box I don't know just don't know. He reeled into the corridor.
She shut the door with her foot, put the assortment of bath, cosmetic equipment away, one by one, each into a separate compart-
ment, she hovered over.

Can't find those heads love. She pecked at the objects around her,
some lingered over, others thrust into darker cavities of the cupboard. No heads Ruth. Then open a tin darling. He stood in the
doorway, held a plate of fish, a book. Don't shove my shaving
things in there. Yes yes they must be put away so untidy otherwise.
Razor, shaving brush, stick, soap were swooped on, pushed out of
sight. Looks a bit more civilised at least. She followed him out
into the kitchen, where she moved swiftly from stove to sink. He
opened the book, while balancing the plate of fish. She moved
round him, carrying saucepans, or poised over the stove. Do feed
Bobo darling he's so very hungry poor thing. Mmmmmmm just
a minute I want. . . . Oh dear I suppose I'll have to do it. She
took away the plate, scrutinised the fish, prodded, and placed the
pieces apart. He could have some of this there seems plenty for us.
What good food like that Ruth oh no what a waste. She held a
piece out and let it fall at his feet. He watched the cat gulp every
bit down, until he looked up for more; rubbed against his legs.
Yes we'll go out tomorrow somewhere nice. Not Sherries please
those awful waiters. They're all right Ruth what's wrong with
them always polite service is damned good food's reasonable best
oysters in town too. They subjugate one all the time the way they
look and I'm sure they snigger behind our backs. Of course they
don't you are a silly girlie yes we'll go there and you can have

46

your favourite Hors d'oeuvre then we'll go onto a show or film whatever you like. She handled the fish that seemed to flap beneath her touch. Surely not enough love? Plenty if you think there isn't I'll do some more potatoes. No no don't bother. He closed the book, tucked under his arm. In the corridor he paused, head raised. He strode into the room, picked up the tape recorder, the box of spools, put them down and went to the window, pulled the curtains round himself, face pressed against the pane, he gazed up. Someone at an open window of the flat opposite, sat and stared back, through the fire escape. Someone else moved to and fro behind. His nose wrinkled against the glass. The person opposite closed their window, remained staring out, down, across. Darling where are you dinner's nearly ready be a poppet and set the table —Leon will you? His lips moved across the window, head worked up and down, finger rubbed until a high pitched sound came. What are you doing—what are you doing behind there? She parted the curtains, stood back, hand covered mouth, then steepled against herself as he spun round, stared at her. She went forward, hands fell to her sides, shoulders slightly stooped. Did you say dinner was ready then? She nodded, looked past him at the window. The rain dripped between the fire escape rungs. The only sound. And their breathing. The deeper breath she took before speaking, while he held his, sometimes dived in before she began, or waited for words she decided not to say, when breath escaped through the narrow partition of her mouth. What is it—what's the matter— what did you see? Nothing—nothing Ruth. She pushed past him, peered through the window, covered with traces of finger marks, mouth, patterns gradually broken up by a sudden onslaught of rain. She started back and rushed from the room. Shouting. Words lost in the thud of rain on concrete, iron. Smiling he edged again nearer the window, which he pushed up a little, and leaned there. Some rain blew in, fell on his face. He pulled the window down, drew the curtains, tugged them into neater folds.

She held the cutlery out. Foul weather never seems to give up but perhaps tomorrow—tomorrow. She handed the knives and forks over to him. So cold in this room too. She always said it was. Your face is filthy all smudged Leon. Where? She dabbed with a handkerchief at his nose, cheeks. He bent towards her, hands knotted behind his back. O.k. that's all right surely now? She licked the handkerchief, and worked it over his face. She stood back, breathed heavily. There that's better now for heaven's sake set the table or everything will be spoilt. They moved towards the door, heads thrust forward. They stepped quickly into the corridor.

In silence they ate. Their faces merged with the shadows, the light of two candles shielded by their glass holders. A record of monks singing, rose and fell, harboured by the walls, her fixed smile, his murmurs between mouthfuls. The music suddenly stopped, he attended to the player, turned knobs, lifted, unscrewed, swore under his breath. She placed inedible pieces of fish carefully on the side of her plate, quietly, methodically she ate. Her face occasionally leaned towards the candlelight. He pushed the player away, switched the radio onto full volume. Food attacked with spear-like movements, he turned the pages of a book. Do you have to have it so loud darling? News—must hear the news find out if they've picked up any more bodies. Bodies? She shrank back and lowered her fork. Black leather part of her hair. Oh yes of course those poor souls what a dreadful thing at least we ought to be thankful for living in a temperate climate. Paper stated a hundred dead wonder how many the radio will say usually differs. Might go well over two thousand an eruption like that. He pierced a piece of fish, which he stared at. What's wrong don't you like it then? She leaned across, inspected his plate, his face in the space between the candles. They glared at each other for a moment, until he swallowed the fish, until the plate was empty. You haven't left any remains for poor Bobo. Bloody animal's had his share Ruth. No need to swear. She collected the plates and marched from the room. He lit his pipe, stretched his legs out, marked a passage in the book. Do you know I nearly brought three plates in—strange. He continued reading, marking, pipe held down, away from him. Darling did you hear? What—what was that? I said I nearly brought. . . . Shhhhhh here's the News. . . . Three plates in. Three—why three —there I knew there would be more that makes nearly two hundred dead and several hundred still missing. Only realised what I'd done when I came out into the corridor. Done what Ruth? Brought three plates. Did you love? He switched the programme over until some light music drifted over them, their shadows that climbed into monumental positions, surveyed the room. She spooned some jelly up, a large lump wobbled as she passed over to him. He rapidly jotted in the margins of the book. She scooped the jelly up into three quick mouthfuls. Rocked, nursed herself with her arms, made a cigarette perform in the ash-tray arena, finally pushed it into the middle until ash scattered over. He grunted, stopped his margin jottings, his lips moved. She stripped the cigarette stump of its paper, sprinkled the tobacco through her fingers. Don't you want your pudding then Leon? Yes yes love in a minute—oh it's jelly isn't there any fruit? No eat it up. You know I'm not keen on jelly love. Very well. She sighed, picked his plate up. Oh all right give it here I don't mind. Yes you do—doesn't matter the woman can have it for lunch tomorrow. But I do want it love. He put his pipe, book aside, reached out as she put the jelly on a spoon. There not so bad is it he likes it really good for him have some more. He opened his mouth, waited, eyes raised. She smiled, brought the spoonful of jelly towards him. Oh there look what you've done oh really Leon. They looked at the jelly slither on the carpet between them. She knelt, scraped the jelly onto a plate. He collapsed in a chair, swung from side to side. Get a cloth darling—ohhhhhh what a mess. She sat on the carpet, stared at the stain. The cloth between his finger and thumb, he bent towards her. Well if you think I'm going to wipe up your mess Leon really. He rubbed very slowly, while she stood over him. There's a bit there—no here yes that's it just there here oh here let me have it honestly darling you're so hopeless. She rubbed intently, while he stood back, his fingers twisted round each other. Here take the cloth and wash it out properly the woman comes tomorrow I don't want her to find a horrid sticky cloth and darling do tidy your room up the bed is in an awful state I don't know what she might think seeing it like that.

He hummed as he left the room, swirled the water in the sink, watched it go down, hung the cloth up in its special place. Make some coffee darling while you're there. She picked the cat up, pressed him to her chin, rubbed against him as he licked her face.

She cooed, stretched out on the carpet, kicked her shoes off, and brushed her face against the cat's neck. What's my Bobo wantey then what's my beautiful Bobos wantey he's very pleased with himself isn't he come on then. She lifted him above her, until his paws spreadeagled, claws out, he struggled. Yes he's very pleased with himself isn't my Bobo. She brought him onto her lap, where she pushed him into a lying position, held him by firm caresses over his body, head, tail.

He entered bearing the tray of coffee. Oh do get the little cups darling I do prefer the little ones. But I've got these now love these will do. But it tastes so much better in the little cups. He held a cup out. I want the small ones darling. Her hands again and again kneaded into the cat who loudly purred. Go and get them darling won't you? He marched out, opened cupboards, banged them shut. Can't find them won't these do? She put the cat down, struggled into her shoes and stumbled out.

Each held a corner of the room, cigarette smoke formed a screen between them. They brought their chairs together when the television programmes started. She commented on women announcers' clothes. He shifted around into more uncomfortable positions, hugged his knees, burst into sudden loud laughter. She knitted faster, dropped several stitches. There look what you've made me do I don't see anything very funny in that. For a time he froze into one position, the flash of television and candles darted over him. God look at that fancy a whole city wiped out by a tidal wave fantastic. He crouched in the semi-darkness. She paused with her knitting, sucked the top of the needles, peered through, over her spectacles. We're jolly lucky really most we can expect are floods a few snow falls yet people forever grumble about this country I think we ought to be thankful for small mercies. She clicked the needles together. Still those tides are dangerous she should have known that. But darling she did. Did what? Know about the currents I mean that's why. . . . But we can't be sure. Pretty certain I mean how could it be otherwise? Oh I don't know I just don't know Christ look at all those people damned lucky we help them with food and clothes. What's on the other programme darling? Nothing much. Well I'm turning in feel quite tired and don't leave your door open Leon you make such a noise in the morning even with my ear plugs I can hear you and do switch your light out I found it still on the other day. She straightened a cushion, gathered up the cat and knitting. Devil of a lot of money rebuild a whole city still they do it so quickly these days too bloody fast really blow on them they'd all fall down can't blame them I suppose question of posterity now hardly relevant. Oh we are morbid to-night there are some clean pyjamas on the top shelf of the airing cupboard. What going to bed already love? He knocked his pipe on the edge of the armchair. Don't do that darling does spoil it so. She balanced the cat on her shoulder, bundled the knitting up. You going to do some work now? Yes think so just a little. Don't forget to switch the fire off when you finish. He nodded, picked up a newspaper, which he covered his face with. Goodnight then darling. Nighty night love. She stared at him, at the newspaper for a moment before leaving.

He lowered the paper, switched the television off, and stood in the middle of the room. Sound of water, doors, Ruth's voice. Her footsteps near. Nearer. He picked up a book. Where did you put her journals darling? Still in the bedroom aren't they? In yours Leon have you been reading them then? Good God no practically impossible her writing so illegible takes an age to wade through a page. I'd like to look anyway go and fetch them darling. She leaned against the door. He approached, hands came up, placed on her shoulders, further down. She pushed him, hands away. I'm tired Leon don't feel—don't darling not now not. . . . Why not you're not unwell? Because—because. . . . Oh very well. Get the journals will you please?

He held out two or three exercise books. There's a life here all right. Some life if you can't even read them Leon. I prefer to listen. Still it's difficult to follow the way she says things well I'll leave you to get on with your work don't stay up too late you're so grouchy the next day when you do and don't forget the lights and fire darling. He nodded, watched her tuck the journals under her arm. Her nightdress caught in the door. It's all right I'll do— I said I'll do it no Leon nooooooh. He whispered, nudged, pushed himself against her, tongue and teeth against the door as she averted her head. I told you Leon. . . . But love. . . . No perhaps tomorrow —tomorrow darling. She pulled at her nightdress. He watched her back, neck, head disappear. His hands hung in front.

He moved slowly, quietly into the other room, sat before the tape recorder, pressed down, turned the volume on low, and watched the silent reel spin. Clearing his throat, he brought the microphone close to his mouth.

She climbed onto the bed, arranged the pillows, stroked the cat, who crawled in beside her. She opened one of the exercise books, adjusted her spectacles, reached for a cigarette and began to read.

March

Today but what day? Nevertheless a day, a time. In Spring. Air, sounds, odours remind. Last night emerging. Confronted by a place. Two people. I to them—they to me? Objects in the room placed as seats in an auditorium. They must be rearranged. No key to the door which automatically opens, closes. Cat aware of this. The cat R adores, L ignores. His body arched, L sidles corners, corridor. First to stride forward with a firm handshake. R shrinks into a former self, peers from there, waits for him to step back. Then out, clutched at, carried down to a level she alone breathes, feels safe in. He crawls over the edge, intake of breath as he lowers a string of formalities. I remained subdued. Concerned smiles, their concern in outbidding each other. We want to make you as comfortable as possible—are you sure you're not cold—too hot perhaps? He leans over, neck twists until the joints crack to his satisfaction. There's a double mattress say if you want an extra blanket won't you. She caressed the eiderdown, while he bounced on the bed. How are you feeling now?

Feeling—feelings? What would it mean to them what has been will be?

When did I begin to construct a moment ago or a space as between waking and dreaming? Patterns reshaped in a form already designed shall anticipate all alternatives, become a measure of a certain consistency. The space between is no less significant than the place occupied at the time. My certainty shall be their confusion.

Weekend spent at their house facing an empty stretch of coastline, which belongs to them up to a certain breakwater. Beyond are the bottles, cartons, orange peel, banana skins, sanitary towels, stockings, contraceptives, gloves, boots, spare parts of prams, cars, bicycles, tins, mattresses, dolls, occasionally a chair that needs just upholstering. L continues a correspondence with the County Council, his father began, to bring into force a law that litter must not be thrown here. Their own notices pulled down, chalked over with obscenities, thrown into the front garden, hung through statues, stuck in flowerbeds.

The house is called The Grey House. It is off-white, appertaining to a Georgian era, but built in the early twenties. The garden spreads, unfolds to the cliff edge where wooden steps lead to the sands occupied by herons and gulls.

On arrival a woman by the river collected sticks, followed by swans. They cried, at least I thought they cried, but it was the woman who shrieked at them, head shook to their twisting forward, following the curve of her back. L rushed to the top of the steps, shouted, fists thrust out. The woman obviously deaf, only the swans stopped in their tracks, wings spread, craning upwards. The beach was deserted. Steps covered in seaweed, small pebbles.

Tide on the turn when after lunch we went down. I walked ahead, or ran into the wind laughing, turned round and waved. L sometimes responds, R never does. I reached the boundary line that lies in wait more to devour the sea than be devoured. High and long in sea-marked stone and brick it shelters, amazes, puzzles those who come down for weekends, a fortnight, staying at the holiday camp a mile and a half away. So they say. I haven't yet seen anyone. It's too early in the year. Season hasn't started yet wait until Easter though. They warn. R nods. L bites his lips, mouth compressed, expands only when looking at himself.

I climbed onto the breakwater, faced a clear straight horizon. Sun half-way held, waves broke in uneven succession further along the coast, where more breakwaters cut up the shore, dark blocks over sand and sea. Thin layers of spray brought surfaces reflecting the sky, in parts oval shaped, like eggs, between rocks. At times the sun focused shallow pools.

When sure they must have approached near enough I turned, they had not progressed from where I had left. They faced each other, R motionless, face tilted forward. L, his back to the sea, gestured. Fingers when released take on a life of their own, circles, angles drawn in the air. Suddenly R's hand came out. So quickly, even now I am unsure whether or not she hit him. Though on replacing the scene action is almost frozen to the extent when the episode is squared off, clipped into a compact picture. Her hand covered one side of his face. A gesture, an embrace perhaps. For I think he caught her arm, made her face him again. I called out, but the wind wrenched the words, flung them into the dark eddies that issued from the green-stained breakwater. When I looked again L walked by the edge of the sea. R sat on the steps. I see her now with hands cupped under chin. Then I think she had one arm balanced on the step above. I took my shoes, stockings off, moved carefully to the end of the breakwater, until parallel with L who stopped, arm lifted, shielding the light from his eyes, or did he wave? I held my stockings up, watched them weave into flying fish above my head. From a round iron framework gushed the sewage water, circled into mucous masses, grafted onto driftwood that bumped against rocks, or stranded in oblong heaps between the alluvium which now and then shifted as though by some underground motivation.

Coldness of the sea brought a kind of numbness, but I stayed until L was near enough. He appeared to shudder, was it from coldness the thought of coldness, or perhaps the sight the other side where rubbish dribbled between rocks? Where some children, who at first I hadn't seen, the objects around, those they played with, so large. No sooner had one construction fallen, or been pushed over, than another was quickly put together. They played in silence, stood back every so often and viewed what had been done, or what next to do. L looked at my feet. He seems equivocal, locked in some quiet confusion of his own. I told him to take his shoes off too. He frowned, said it was cold, getting late, pointed at the lowered sun, and marched back, without looking round. I retraced his footsteps until the sea made this impossible.

Mantis-like I hang over many desultory designs, toy with subterfuges. Attempts at censoring any desire to think what should be felt. This the most difficult. So conditioned are the reflexes they become part of a mausoleum, when emotions outweigh surrounding matter a figure monstrous in shape chiselled from soft substances. When thought is chipped out, thrown as titbits for those who look on. Waiting.

How begin to find a shape—to begin to begin again—turning the inside out: find one memory that will lie married beside another for delight? Seems beyond attainment.

Habits. Their habits fallen into easily. Perversely. Today R's birthday. L gave her two goldfish, he continually feeds, peers at, chases the cat away from their glass tank, which at first leaked.

A few friends invited for dinner. Couples R knew prior to her marriage. Before the guests arrived L reached a near hysterical pitch. Nothing seemed right, everything had to be changed, reversed, rearranged. Furniture. Food. Records, books, magazines. Lighting. Paintings. Position of the goldfish tank. R changed dresses several times. I borrowed one. She tried on all her jewellery, wept at her hair until she listened to my reassurances.

Before the guests arrived we sat in the room that sank in that dark, or wielded under the light projected from the corners. Shadow players emerged, indifferent to each other's interpretations on revolving stages, swinging them perhaps together, or out into space. I waited, listened for their words to break up the little areas of chosen colour they worked at from bases they had secured.

Then they came. Two by two. Incriminating each other's appearance by a point by point investigation. Only when the last guest hadn't turned up did L succumb to the evening's entertainment. Performed with R a defiant, unapproachable, unity. Everyone immediately concerned in being, doing what is expected of them. As if given the choice of two packs of cards to set the pace, but were misled by an invisible third.

L at the head of the table rubbed his hands, chuckled as a boy with thoughts of some prank he and the other men might hatch. Hissed between sentences, waited, hoped for the others to take their cue. Usually taken up by an 'ex-flame' of R's, with calculated eloquence. In French. Italian. Cigars pampered, liqueur glasses stroked—the stems. Becoming benevolent in arguments as the atmosphere grew warmer, dense with smoke, drowsed by low music and candlelight.

I heard myself talk, laugh. Erect at the table. Sweep in and out of the room. And dance. I wanted to get high, but not higher than anyone else. R seemed anxious, as though something had been forgotten, fussed as a child with new dolls, making sure each of us sat in appropriate places. L dedicated himself to the moment, person, subject. R smiles only when he pauses, touches her necklace, bracelets, rings. Glances at the women, estimating. If L should stray in any one direction for too long she asks for a cigarette, refuses all offers except his. While he continues talking, punctuates words by drawing diagrams in the air, on the table; flicks the lighter long after use. R takes refuge in displaying her false nails and, in between mouthfuls of delicacies, exchanged reminiscences before marriage, her repertoire never exhausted, making a confidant out of whoever she chose should listen. I was placed next to her.

This afternoon half a fossil discovered, intaglio, cut from a rock, cool against my cheek. My hands. Against his.

A long walk with L by the river to a hill, where out of breath we lay flat on our backs. I noticed the moistness gather on his hands, forehead, the intensity of his eyes, blue, like small stones discovered after scraping away dozens of prosaic pebbles. We made some kind of conversation, can't remember exactly what, except about a French book L thought very good. I agreed enthusiastically. Once back he pounced on a book, declared, almost triumphantly, that it hadn't been the one he had spoken about.

Friday

My hands instruments of torture. Hers butterflies, when excited, flustered. His feed the goldfish. Fingers snap like crickets in long grass, as he enters, leaves a room.

His face in the car mirror. Panic. The speedometer jerks up, back, up again, further round, a feeler once an appetising victim found, hovers, then pulls quickly to the nest.

Sunday

All afternoon surrounded, exchanging newspapers. I came across the following:

'I was camp adjutant, I merely sat in my office with my paper-work. It may sound unbelievable, but I never set foot inside the actual camp.'

'Did you never make any attempt to find out about the 60,000 human beings locked in there? Did they have shelter? How were they fed? Was there a water supply?'

'I never heard of any complaints.'

'Who was able to complain?'

'No one was allowed inside. It was punished by death!'

'Look at the map, look at that grey building, that yard. Did you know about that?'

'No. No.'

'Did you not know that there were three gallows in that yard?'

'Three what?'

'GALLOWS. Gallows from which men were hanged.'

'I didn't see them from my window.'

'Did it never dawn on you that there was something very, very wrong?'

'I asked no questions. I was careful.'

'What did you do when people were beaten to death?'

'It did not come to my knowledge.'

'Did you never hear of the so-called rabbit-chase?'

'No.'

'Did you never hear that people were driven into the barbed wire fence and shot?'

'I don't recall anything of the kind.'

'Was the Commandant ever dissatisfied with you?'

'Well, there was the paper shortage, I had my own way of folding the economy envelopes. He was furious with me.'

'What did you think these camps were for?'

'Where the enemies of our country were being re-educated.'

'Did you see the lists with arriving prisoners' names?'

'There were such lists.'

'Did you know that some names had a black cross put against them?'

'I seem to recall that.'

'Did you know what the black cross meant?'

'No. No.'

'It meant Return Undesirable. Did you know about the standing cells? About the gravel pit? Did you know that the rations were calculated to keep a man alive for a maximum of three months?'

'No. No. No.'

'Did you know there were gas-chambers?'

'Yes. But I had no occasion to speak about them.'

'Never to your Commandant?'

'He was a strange unapproachable man. I avoided asking him questions.'

'Did you know what Special Treatment meant?'

'Special Treatment was Murder! I was profoundly upset about it.'

'Did you know that there was a standing rule that all children up to sixteen were to be gassed with their mothers?'

'I never saw any children, I was ill, wretchedly so at the time, I was helpless, if I'd reported it I would have written my own sentence. I only took note of it all from the outside. It was not my concern. It was the task of the Political Section.'

Monday

A recognisable nausea provokes the desire to become something in their lives, anything. Everything. But whose move is the next?

While L was away for a few days one of the goldfish died. R put it in a neighbour's dustbin. L returned, paused in the doorway, looked round, as though sounding the place, making sure the territory is exactly as he left it. He didn't notice the missing goldfish until the other one pined away. L didn't speak for a day. He became completely unapproachable.

Friday

I weave through patterns on walls; branches shake in the wind, lift up and down beside the bed—their shadows. Murmurs next door. When going to the bathroom I can hear what is said. Tonight startled by my own reflection a carved face in the middle of a stone wall, looking again difficult to find.

Innumerable hours going over the day's actions, reactions, leading into an enclosure a tent finally collapses in the darkness; silence egged on by their movements. Their silence. Thoughts somersault, until dizzy I fall asleep.

Speculation in assuming a love for a substitute absorbed me long before suspecting it of myself; capabilities yes, being a good mimic, emotions are loopholes for self-expressions, if others are willing to play along, it becomes comparatively simple. Days of exultation, but moments of cross-sectioned feelings. How can I explain, reveal all, arrive at some kind of clarity? Supplant these huge areas of unspoken thoughts. Their voices. Wish-fulfillment—revenge?

Tuesday
Oblivion with all the doors open. Walk into their room. Lie on her bed. His. Confront the mirror. R's latest lipstick, dress, hats at all angles. Her wardrobe on one side full of toys. Huge teddy bear with an eye missing. Pity she doesn't keep a diary. Letters immediately destroyed—an animal covering its tracks. Pursued by a compulsion to jeopardise such a bourgeois stronghold. So often scorned before, but soon understood, almost succumbed to: an ambiguous luxury, with them an inherent instinct.
Here my dreams can be interrupted. Window overlooks fire escape, when open the squeaks, crash of lift. L's steps. R's more difficult to discern. Door kept half open by a chair I see the parquet flooring of their room, edge of bookshelves. L's books on art, archaeology, encyclopaedias, handed down. In childhood having no playmates, his stepmother wouldn't allow, so books became his sole companions. In regal state he played, dreamed alone. Relationships hardly comprehended for a long time no place in the world he had recreated. Even now he has the charm of a small boy

brought suddenly into a roomful of adults, rubs his eyes, blinks round, unsure whether he still dreams or is awake. He has, in fact, just turned forty, hair thinning, but retains a fairness; blond hairs above collar, wrists. R uses auburn rinses, hair carefully coiled, nape of her untanned neck exposed, cultivated for her own nourishment, she bends, feels the light must fall just there, and waits for his touch. Of the two he flirts the more, though an unstudied approach. R conscious the whole time, aware of a hand, eye, jumps to hasty conclusions. Blushes easily—did you notice how long he held my hand—or why does he always look in my direction when kissing that child of theirs? L strokes his nose, bringing attention to the whimsical expression under his eyes, the way his arms, legs stretch out—a Gulliver becoming an easy prey in other places outside his own.

A time ago I was more vulnerable to my own reactions, responses, taking into account only what others might say, voice inflections, gestures dismissed. But after a series of mime lessons, with masks, I realised how much can be interpreted by mere movement. How easy it is to camouflage with a flux of innuendoes. The habitual nervousness of animals, but never so predictable.

I become almost a shadow. The kind that extends up the wall, across the ceiling, dwindles gradually into other larger shadows. In my room. Theirs. Occasionally they invite me to listen to a concert on the radio. We lie mummified, unaccountable inches apart on the brass four-poster, heads turned away, eyes closed, the touch of slippery eiderdown. Their warmth. Sound of R's bracelets. Usually two concerts at least a week. I remember at the convent love was imagining what lay behind Christ's loin cloth. This is no less imagining. But a situation I long to wade in right up to the very limits of imagination if possible. Gain another level, an added dimension, preferably bringing them both with me. How far can the emotions stretch though? However for the time being I ask of nothing else but to be, live as they live.

If I'm up first I take the tea in. R terrified of creatures suddenly flying in, feels sure they will drop down, crawl over her face in the dark, so she keeps the window shut. I noticed the other day when she pulled back the curtains, a mole under her right arm, under the left a mark from the last abscess. She shuddered as the light tumbled in.

L delights in slow-motioning the agony of being roused from some exciting dream, recounted later, elaborated with gestures as he goes along. Quickens as our horror mounts, grunts with approval as we attempt to match each other's interpretations.

Thursday

To see their cotton wool faces, zipper mouths expand, shrivel, contract. To throw their salt-cellar out of the window, drill through their sound-proofed walls.

This evening they had a row and L stormed out. R's voice a siren, lowered only at the sound of the lift. L had left all the doors open. Had he changed his mind? We both paused, heads lifted, waiting. She muffled herself with a cushion. I stroked her hands. We giggled later over tea and cakes until L returned. His breath smelt of whisky and French cigarettes.

Emotions handled, shifted about, dropped, picked up, but always attached as a child's pair of gloves.

Another weekend. We went riding on a bright morning, leaving L to attend his orchids. We turned and waved, but he was preoccupied, stooped over in the summerhouse. We laughed, bent over the horses' withers. R's hair mingled with her horses's mane. I was in front most of the way towards the house. Fast oh faster R cried as L emerged and crossed the garden. We're going down to race come and watch. She shouted. He waved as we bounced down the bank onto the sand. I heard R laugh, shriek behind. Aware that L stood on the steps. A child waved a kite on the breakwater, which the wind caught up and then it fell, heaved towards us. The horses shied, bolted towards the sea. Looking round I saw R had fallen off. She rolled over, made to get up, then crumpled as L approached.

All day, and the next, she lay in a darkened room, between migraine pills she cried, groped for L's arms, or mine. We ate with her, perched either side of the bed, and whispered. She moved as though under water, her head raised up, hands flapped over the crest of blankets, sheets. L's head jerked—a bird's beak making strange noises. Any titbits thrown in his direction are not immediately swallowed, but stored, while searching for something he feels owing. The flick of hands, pale yellow fleck in his eye. His gardening boots he kept on while R was ill, with months of earth clinging to them—white marks as if someone had chewed them bit by bit.

R remained in the upstairs room for two days, her face filled out, eyes bright. We surrounded her with cushions, magazines, fruit, sweets, and moved in the television, which we watched, lying either side of her.

Redolence of the sick-room. Crepuscular movements of those in attendance. In abeyance. Then she decided to get up and sat, half-hidden by rugs, in the garden. L presented her with a hamster, which they let out onto the table at meal times. Last night R seemed determined to recall their honeymoon, probably because it was their anniversary. A monologue about the time spent abroad, traipsing around museums, churches, and something about a girl L still corresponded with at the time, sent poems to. He remained, silent stared at the hamster's manoeuvrings between our plates and the cage. It stored in cheek-pouches huge pieces of toast until its small yellow body bulged either side. It scuttled back into the cage, vomited the food into the nest for future meals. Once or twice I looked at L as R ambled on, his eyes seemed glazed, or perhaps it was the light, as he closed the cage door, and we watched the hamster on its hind legs claw the bars.

Today I came across L's diary. Days of headaches, appointments, library, dinner and lunch engagements. Nothing very much apart from some little black crosses, which seem to be some kind of code. I spilt some coffee over the desk, some trickled onto a page. I wiped it carefully, but there was still a slight mark. Immediately visited with fears, crazy thumping ones caught up with those choking ones when a child stealing apples, flowers, or the silver threepenny bits out of the box Mother kept, but there were so many she'd hardly notice a few missing? I little realised she checked now and then, fully accounted for those put in the Christmas pudding. Would it have been best if I had torn the page out, he might not notice. A page with two of the black crosses though? I put the diary back in the drawer, took it out again, flipped through, the page was definitely marked. I rubbed the stain until the paper became thin, thinner, my hands hot, until I heard the lift. I pushed it back, and haven't dared look again.

In R's cupboard I discovered some photos of a girl, something about them reminds me of R, yet they are not her, the features are entirely different. But I will have to look again. What is it exactly, the way the girl stands, shoulders slightly hunched, the tilt of her head? R has no sister. Perhaps some relative? It is curious how they fascinate me. I must ask if she has any family photos.

April
How far can an obsession stretch—colour the imagination?

Evenings by the log fire, mist hangs low, patches of ground are Chinese islands. Regions explored that are sparked off by a certain light, or air. Countries visited, those yet to see. Times when vowing I shall remember this now, which are never so real as those flashes—a door unexpectedly opens upon an unfamiliar scene, until gradually certain landmarks are retrieved. Nostalgia almost experienced at the time, the knowledge in that moment of something never going to be exactly the same again. The image frozen. As standing in a lift going neither up nor down.

Saturday

At my suggestion L made a platform, with steps leading from either side, in the empty swimming pool. We both write little scenarios, which R half-heartedly joins in. We improvise as we go along. My favourite one with the masks is just the three of us, two reject one, or one rejects two, or all three reject each other, or equally accept. L brought some of the statues down, arranged in rows, facing the platform. We mimed, sang, danced between, flinging some flowers, old clothes over the bronze and metal pieces of sculpture, a few without heads. It seems to delight L every time we can get away and go down there. Sometimes just the two of us, exchange masks, hide behind the statues, pretend making love to them, and L's laugh loud, louder until darkness drives us out, back to the house.

It was Easter Monday, or the Sunday, when the three of us performed a mime play, I had sketched out, when I became aware of shadows, other than our own, moving along the interior of our sunken theatre. I looked up and saw two faces over the edge, hands held across their mouths. R and L continued their gestures, moved around each other, unaware of our audience, then pellets of earth showered over us. L brushing himself down, ran up the steps, swayed at the top. Must have been some creature, the cat, some animal digging a hole. He concluded. There were footprints near the flowerbeds, which I covered over.

Mid-week

Doors swing in the wind. Ladder. Half a ladder against the summerhouse. Spider on the wall. Feet tucked in. A place where stars are stars, and windows are glass. After all.

High up in a hotel room, that faced a vast stretch of moor, where the mist rose, sank, and rose again, fingered the windows. Cupboard full of crooked hangers, hung the wrong way. Informed the place was full, however it proved empty apart from ourselves. The sheets white, but yellow. The waiter shuffled endlessly along corridors. Once while in the bathroom I sensed someone looking in when I stepped out of the bath. I felt it must be L, but in the mirror, the old waiter's sunken face, tongue rested on dry lips, pink eyes attached to mine. Later he hovered between our beds, reluctant to leave until L brusquely repeated that's all thank you. My knees, bones next to the lumps of mattress. I listened to unfamiliar noises, silence. R's breathing. L's nasal gasps, restless turnings. Until the light crept in, mutterings of birds began, then only then did I stop periodically holding my breath, and play around the idea of sleepwalking, never really getting further than the space separating my bed from theirs. But suppose a nightmare? Scream, run over, fling myself on L's bed, but immediately confronted by his face looming up in the glare of the bedside lamp, hand out as if a moth had flown in, gently caught, opening the window and R saying it's all right, go back now, you'll be all right, tell us all about it in the morning.

In silence we ate in the empty dining-room. Heavy ornate furniture like ancient kings and queens, hostile at having their kingdom invaded. While the waiter stood by the hatchway, watched us eat. Later I saw him cross the moor with two huge dogs on leads. At lunch he served with shaky hands, bloodshot eyes. R decided nothing was right, and the waiter trotted in, out, coughing or cringed by the hatchway, while we sipped coffee, brandies. L judiciously ordered more, and attempted to tell funny stories. That reminded me of the weekend meetings with my father, when there should have been acknowledged pauses, he embarked on a long story, chuckled over, and prodded me to join in. I see him now, not very tall, suspicion of a paunch, cramming a dead match into the box of other dead matches. Look at his watch, and rush to the station hours before due to depart. Where I enlarged on the conspiracy of not being his daughter, perhaps his mistress, bend close over the buffet table, stir cold tea, and be emotional over Mother. Later met by her, waiting behind the barrier, with that look of a lover, accusative, yet ready, so willing to forgive. Having to relate in detail of the day spent, and all I could remember were the jokes. But at night in the room next to hers, I heard his laughter, saw him relight his pipe, brush the tobacco off his tweed trousers.

When we left the hotel I saw the waiter pause from wiping the crumbs off the table, come to the window. The dogs barked somewhere, as we banged the car doors, and sped away down the drive, lined with poplars. The hotel shrank into mist. We took a wrong turning, spent hours looking for signposts, stopped to read the map. While mist gathered thicker around, over us. L's voice became louder, R grew quieter. We ended back at the hotel, staying another night. The table we had previously already laid. We asked for separate rooms, but the proprietor explained they were short of staff, and as the room we had already shared was prepared. . . . After dinner L and I played chess, while R looked at magazines. In the corridors, hallways, mist wrapped over everything, everywhere clocks ticked. The waiter shuffled about, with dandruff on his shoulders, back, yellow round his mouth like pollen. His back bent as he brought the cocoa in. When he left our room I did not hear him shuffle away, at times I thought I heard the sound of keys, a slight wheezing. Like the times Auntie M was caught outside the lounge door, she didn't have to bend to the keyhole. My greatest ambition at five was to be taller than her, tall enough to open doors myself. Her wagging finger I still see, her teeth clicking in between

mouthfuls of bread and butter dipped in tea. Sometimes she dared
to have some cherry brandy, or elderberry wine, if my father was
home resting, or about to go on tour again. She sat at the end of
the round table, the cracked end, on the edge of her chair, feet off
the ground, wiping remains from around her mouth, where fuzz
like ash grew. She never ate much at our table, but later I saw her
take the tin box out of the larder, and paper bags filled with
biscuits, cakes, sweets, she hoarded, took to bed and nibbled. Which
Mother objected strongly to because of the mice; crumbs all over
the floor and bed that mingled with mouse droppings, were seen
when searching for the only sharp knife in the house—one with a
broken handle, the one I threatened to kill the girl next door with.

I flung open our door. The waiter disappeared round the
corridor, tails flapped between his bent legs.

Next day, bright, clear, and the moor folded out into molten
lead, as we spun by the edge onto roads that dipped, danced with
light, strange white hypnotic light that comes through forests. The
sun a mushroom, sprang from the thick growth, caught the leaves
into metallic surfaces. Deer, surprised, leaped away into darker
recesses, as L turned the radio up, and R laughed, saying look oh
look ohhhhhhh look at that did you see it—did you see that—oh
how lovely do look? L bent lower over the wheel, applied the
brake when turning corners. His face pale in the mirror, but his
eyes bright, fixed on the road ahead, cursed anyone who might
get in front, burrowed out, back again, when he wished to pass.
They had an argument as to where we should stop off to eat. From
town to town, until we came to a small seaside resort where everything was shut, apart from a cramped coffee bar. We sat on high
stools, and avoided looking in the mirror.

Confronted by words, names, dates. A jigsaw, secretly known
off by heart, but tossed about, making it harder to piece together
—which piece fits in precisely where? Causing conflict, when
there's almost the desire to opt out. And if I did—what?

Absurdity?

A book. On the fly-leaf, inscribed with L's recognisable horizontal writing: For you with love from me in remembrance of that day in June. I turned the page over, a few more, put the book down, opened it again, stared at the inscription. Which June, what day, why? A time possibly when I knew neither of them—beginning of a hot summer perhaps, when they first met, made love? The volume still in uniform cover. A few pages dog-eared but retains that newness—the smell of gum—or washing dried in the sun.

Last night they took me to a party, held by some friends. Half way through, when the room was packed, I looked round for R. I made a tour of the house, went down to the second floor, and was about to enter a room when I heard R's confiding tone, insistent, persuasive. In the corridor there were some books, I took one down, and listened. The man's voice low, but he spoke very little apart from saying ah yes, no, or why was that? As R went on I realised the mystery of the photographs was solved—they were of herself before having her face altered by plastic surgery. I squatted with the open book, and now and then looked through the doorway at R reclined on the sofa, the man leaned over from an armchair. I could not see R's face, how I longed to in that moment, as she went on describing why she had wanted to change her features. But do you now consider yourself any more beautiful than nature made you? the man asked. Yes I think so, besides I don't see why we can't choose to be what we want when nowadays the facilities are provided. But how unsure of yourself you must have been did it change you as person? I think so. She gave here one of her abrupt laughs, which indicated she was getting bored, wanted the subject changed. Or perhaps she was just uneasy. A movement on the stairs, I saw L come down, balancing two drinks. Does he know?

When we returned slightly drunk to the flat, I stared hard at R's face. The skin in places tight, around the mouth a certain pressure, maybe that is why she doesn't smile very often. Reminded me, when a child, I stripped white flowers to see the layers of yellow juicy green underneath. L played at being more drunk than he actually was, which annoyed R intensely, especially when he pretended to be jealous of the time she'd spent with the stranger at the party. She locked her door. L poured out some more drinks, put some jazz records on, and we danced, until R stood sniffing in the doorway, cheeks smudged with mascara. L swayed, laughing, pushed her into his room, and closed the door. I heard them giggle, like children over a well-known game, slightly guilty at the thought of being found out. Rising in that pleasure. Then the silence.

In the dark, the outline of the fire escape, I choose the nights spent in shared fantasies. Of other places, and places that replace boundaries of bed, floor, walls. A cliff edge, the sea spilling into sky. Back to front. Kneeling. Like dogs. He said. Arms stretched out, bodies arched, more submission demanded. And rolling over as in waves. With the waves. That later came. Kept coming. I want to fuck you on stairways, in telephone booths, in public places. Tie you up, and let them all see you, fuck you, do what they will, and whip you, lick you, and fuck you again. A whole line of us fucking, like a train rushing through the darkness. And he put spittle on my nipples, made me feel them as well—buds sticky with rain. We'd lie in a warm wetness, and all day the odour, his, mine, like water, flowers have been taken out of. Contained in those smells, movements, words. Sense of touch as trees in a high wind, or remaining conspicuously upright, solitary afterwards. But wait. Lap in the hot air, the hardness, softness. Low laughter into cries. Never the same pattern no matter how many times. Rhythms suggested varied aspects of each other. Rest in some, encourage the speed of others. There seemed no limit. In approach. Counter-approach. Retraction only to be forced over the edge. Hung. Looked into as a mango fruit torn open. Expanded. Dripping.

White, wet, gleaming from the pile of bedclothes. Clothes in heaps, dotted as islands risen from an eruption. In the morning easing ourselves onto each other, half asleep. Feelers. Tongues found nests, shells. Early light dipped between, the greyness sank into the ground. Fingers clutched revolving suns. Moons reflected a slippery surface of an area rediscovered. Crawled out of each other's ribs, buried half digested tensions. A world could be as small as the navel. Armpit. Crevices equally explored, marvelled at. Expression of a dance that takes its own course. Strung in space, other spaces acquired, as grains of sand shifted only by incoming tides. A cave unwillingly crept from, and discovering the light too much. Marked our own impressions on interior walls. Signs pursued relentlessly, as floating in one stream of light thrown upon an otherwise darkened sea. Hairs in the mouth—strands of seaweed. Spray on skin. Fingertips. Touched down, settled between rocks, only air and warmth waited for, to dry us.

Narrow dimensions of theirs catch me up into an appalling lethargy, when anything would be welcome as a release. They swing each other against walls that bounce them back into themselves.

This afternoon an old bag in the back of R's wardrobe. Expected perhaps letters, fingers contacted something soft, like animal fur, turned out to be hair—masses of dark hair.

Tuesday
R's osteopath called round, I was about to leave the room as she

undressed, but she asked me to remain, bring up a chair, sit next to her. Strange to see her half naked, breasts larger than I had realised. She moaned, groaned, as the osteopath pummelled and pulled. The more she groaned, the more he seemed to smile, nod, breathe heavily, panted over her, as she twisted at times away from his touch. Her eyes rolled, a trickle of blood on chin from her bitten lips. The osteopath techniquely resolute. Sharp but heavy movements, manner. I was surprised to hear afterwards that his hands wandered further than necessary—but of course, he never admits it R hastily added perhaps not even to himself, and he wouldn't have done anything while you were with us. She suggested I undergo some treatment—it makes you feel wonderful a couple of days later. What struck me at the time was the quiet determined efficiency of the osteopath when asking for his fee; the cheque looked at several times, which brought back the faces of the psychiatrists so vividly, behind their huge mahogany desks, while I spun, enlarged on childhood, love-life, why I didn't believe in having the baby adopted. They knowing as much as I did that whatever I said didn't really matter, as long as the money was to hand, it being already fixed. But the prolonged game continued, where the set questions came, a sermon on adoption, contraception, endlessly repeated. They seemed to gain almost a perverse satisfaction from enquiring how many men I had in fact slept with in the past year. Confessions they obviously grew parasitical about, as much as the enquiries as to how, where the money for the termination would come from. The words 'traumatic experience' dealt out religiously that would probably be mine to cope with afterwards. But how convey the utter sense of relief of having my body back again related to the mind that functioned in freedom divorced from the computer system they had set up. R is, of course, against such things, the very idea horrifies her. What would her reaction be if she knew? and L's? If they have a child, a boy, they intend calling him Clovis.

R has given up going to the fertility clinic, feeling a specialist might be more helpful. An Indian medium, recommended by a friend, told her she would have a child in two years' time, which consoled her for a while, until she went back to see him, and he

began the session by saying she had two children and would probably marry again. She arranged to see an analyst, who suggested
she had a mother fixation, which made her laugh, as she finds her
mother tyrannical and tiresome. She became self-absorbed, and
only outwardly excited when the time came for her analysis. She
found him fascinating, described him in detail, after each session.
A few days ago she returned noticeably pale, and hardly spoke.
When L enquired why she had given up going for treatment, she
said oh he's not much good really—a waste of money. She's been
very quiet since, refuses all offers to go out, either shopping or even
to the pictures. When L suggested, laughing, that she had been in
love with her analyst, she flew into a temper, shut herself up in the
bedroom with the cat, until dinner, when she announced she
thought another abscess was starting up under her arm, and remained in bed the next day, refused to see the doctor, or for L to
look. I developed a cough, a pain in my chest, which became
awkward as L is impossibly bad-tempered when left to cope. So I
decided to get better, though took great care in adding extra face
powder, and without lipstick the effect produces ample sympathy.
They exclaimed how pale I looked, that perhaps we ought to go
into the country for a long period. An over-all sense of relief now
spreads through the flat as R flies from cupboard to suitcase, and L
packs some books, cancels lunch appointments, and other engagements, sets the alarm clock for an early start tomorrow.

For three days rain. L has spent most of the time with his orchids,
potters about in the summerhouse, a vague look at meal times,
catalogues spread out on the table. While R moves and moves
about the house, changes furniture around, makes long distance
telephone calls to friends she rarely sees in town, asking them to
come down for the weekend. I go for walks along by the shore,
trace footprints to the breakwater, where I shelter, watch the herons
stalk, aristocratic they disregard the gulls. Beyond the breakwater,
and yet another, men pulled nets in, silently, slowly, in a measured

dance of common curiosity. I stood behind, watched them haul for a long time, finally they crowded round the catch, one huge fish leaped into the air, higher than the men's heads, twisted violently, then down, fluttered amongst broken fins, blood in the net, while the men passed round cigarettes, and turned with half-closed eyes to look at me.

Three months now of living with two people and not any nearer—nearer. Tactics flounder before even begun. There seems no answer. And yet. . . .

Ruth bent over some photographs, held negatives up, tore them into little pieces, put them in an ash-tray, and struck a match. Watched the flames lick, the photos curl. She knelt on the bed, where a mirror, brush lay, where the cat slept. She opened the window, emptied the burnt remains, that fluttered, scattered, fell into the street, where newspapers flapped against the gutters. A man in the opposite building gazed across, threw a cigarette out. She drew the curtains, opened the door, listened outside Leonard's room. She tiptoed back, slid under the blankets. Touched herself, the cat, brought him up until his head rested on her shoulder. She stared at the stream of light through the white curtains. Switched the bedside lamp on, held the mirror up, looked at her mouth, re-arranged hair into various styles, made plaits, smiled with mouth open, closed. Tossed the bedclothes aside, took her nightdress off, inspected her breasts, held the mirror to them, licked a finger and rubbed a nipple.

Leonard propped himself up with more pillows, turned pages of a catalogue, coloured photographs of orchids spread out. He pushed them away, brought the blankets over his head, knees up, hands under a pillow. Gazed into darkness. He fumbled for the radio and knocked a glass over, cursing he watched the whisky spread over table, drip onto the carpet, which he wiped with a handkerchief, paused, and looked up. Ruth is that you—Ruth? He opened the door, adjusted his pyjamas, kicked the door shut. Drew back the curtains, stretched his arms out, across the window, head against the pane, eyes closed. Twisted his neck several times, opened the window, looked up, down at the square where pigeons behind railings waddled by the benches, a few chairs had collapsed on the grass, upright iron ones stuck out of the pond. He watched a man put a poster up. An aeroplane passed over, rose higher, left a white trail that disappeared behind the buildings. He scratched his chest, went back to the bed, picked a catalogue up, flicked through, closed. Opened the door. Ruth do you want some tea? He tapped on her door, tried the handle. Asleep? He bent over as she murmured, wriggled, blinked up. Would you like some tea now—I'll make it if you like? Mmmmmm lovely have a good night? Yes not bad and you? Didn't get to sleep until quite late. Reading those journals anything interesting? Difficult as you said the writing is so bad. Discover anything that might . . . Not really—no nothing much—feed Bobo will you Leon while you're up and don't make the tea too strong as you usually do and lots of sugar please. O.k. anything to eat? Some toast would be nice—what's the time? Early newspapers haven't arrived yet—funny smell—burning or something is the electric blanket on Ruth? No here take Bobo. She gathered the cat up, passed him over, he sprang away, jumped back onto the bed. See he hates me that animal. Silly of course he doesn't how can a poor dumb creature hate a human being Leon really bring something in here then for him will you please—please? What have you done to your hair Ruth? Why what's wrong with it? Plaits love for you ah no I mean . . . Keeps it tidy—oh do go and make the tea darling so thirsty. She yawned, pulling the sheet up to her chin, and closed her eyes. He sat on the edge of the bed, looking round the room. She watched him, eyes half-closed, sighed and turned over, rubbing her head against the pillow, the cat. Go on then darling. He leaned over, to touch her neck. She turned suddenly, arm across her face, the other covered her breasts. Sleep without anything on now then? No—no just got rather hot in the night, think I might be in for a cold. Hope not—well. . . . He levered himself off, and left.

She felt under the blankets, slipped on the nightdress, and brushed her hair out. Put the journals in a drawer, but took them out again, and opened one. She began tearing at a page, but placed it back into the drawer as Leonard appeared. They sipped tea, read the newspapers. Chap here killed his wife then committed suicide confessed on tape coroner apparently suggested he couldn't see why they shouldn't accept the recording as evidence. Why'd he murder her then? She kept running about banging doors. God what mad people exist Leon fancy just for that killing the poor woman. The man described by neighbours as level-tempered and very quiet. Ugh usually that type who do such things anyway why you reading such morbid stuff this early darling? Just the tape idea I suppose you know. . . . How many more reels have we left of hers Leon? Two I think. Suppose we ought to run through them in case. . . . Do you think she was in love with you I mean. . . . Good heavens what makes you say that Ruth? Well it's conceivable after all you're attractive lots of young girls look at you I've noticed and don't pretend you hadn't realised that. I wasn't denying it. How long did you in fact know her Leon before—well before I met her? Can't remember actually came to work for me let's see must be a year or so. Did you know she had an abort—abortion? When? Before she came here in fact that's what she had and not the illness we were led to believe. Oh. Is that all you can say Leon? What is there to say I know you don't agree with that sort of thing but she was a practical girl in many ways. He continued reading, turned the pages carefully over. She fell back against the pillows, stared at the folds in the curtains. More tea love? No don't think so. Not too strong I hope? It was all right. What's up Ruth headache again? A bit. Want your pills? No it'll pass. I'll leave you then try and have some more sleep if you can. He kissed her forehead, she put her arms round him. He collapsed on top. Leon Leon ohhhh darling. Yes love? Oh nothing. You smell nice. Don't. . . . Don't what love? My head ah darling don't. . . . I want you Ruthey—Ruth. Ah noooooooh. She shifted away until she hung over the bed, shaking. He lifted her back, parted her legs. No Leon don't not now—not like this. He pressed down, held himself over her face, mouth, between her breasts. Don't cry shhhhhh there. He touched her with his fingers. Leon did you ever make. . . . Shhhhh there you like this don't you like this and this. Her arms spread out, he brought her legs up, until they clutched his back. He twitched several times, then sank down. She lay motionless, tears ran into her mouth. Sorry Ruth I. . . . It's always the same Leon always—get a towel will you? He rolled off. Sorry but. . . . Doesn't matter get that towel one in the drawer there. Not one here love? Get one from the bathroom then. The blanket over her head, she crouched, rocked backwards, forwards, and moved her legs away from the damp parts of the sheet. Here we are shall I dry you? No give it here. She pulled the towel from him and rubbed slowly, then faster between her legs, and over the rest of her body. He stood at the end of the bed, limply, looked on. Away. Face flushed, sweat on his forehead, where the veins had swollen. She pulled the towel out and handed it to him. Well I'll leave you to sleep a little how do you feel? Yes you do that. Ah Ruth. . . . Shrugging he went out.

She looked at the door, walls, paintings, window, and picking up a pillow she threw it at the curtains.

He whistled, while slowly dressing, and squinted into the mirror, inspected his teeth, contemplated the row of ties. He snatched one up, and put it against his shirt, tried another, stretched his neck, grunted, and clipped the tie on. Picked the catalogues up, hesitating over a large picture of a dark maroon-purple orchid, cup-shaped, with innumerable wrinkles, a solitary leaf, rigidly fleshy dark green. Sighing he put the catalogue on the table, turned and faced his reflection.

She patted the eiderdown into place. Opened the drawer, and pulled out a journal, turned several pages, until she came to a blank one. She began writing, paused now and then, sucked the top of the pen, and read what she had written, some she crossed out, then went on quickly, until she reached the bottom of the page, she blotted carefully, closed and put it back in the drawer. In front of the dressing-table she applied foundation cream, powder, pulled her eyelids down and drew a thin black line, curved slightly upwards at each corner, and shaded in some green shadow. She searched a lizard-skin box for a lipstick, opened those that were whittled down, found a scarlet one, which she jabbed onto her upper lip, pressed with her lower lip. Tilting the mirror, she sat upright, looked at the reflection of a photograph on the bureau behind, of herself and Leonard in the vestibule of a church.

He sat by the window, smoking his pipe. Watched the street become more crowded, queues formed either side of the road at the bus stops. The square already filled with women leaning over, away from prams, and old people with sticks hobbled to the benches, brought out crumbs from their pockets, paper bags, and threw to the pigeons. Suddenly he pulled the window up and leaned out, opening his mouth wide, but closed it firmly. He rushed from the room, the flat, swore loudly as the lift gates would not connect at first. He looked left, right, across the road, and ran down the street. At the corner he halted. Then walked slowly back, his head averted from the queue of people who stared at his coatless appearance, slippered feet. Seeing Ruth at the window he waved, but she stepped back. A road sweeper unbent, chuckling. Leonard curtly nodded, swept through the revolving doors, into the lift, where he smoothed his hair, squinted at his dim reflection in the metal surround.

Ruth picked the milk bottles up. What on. . . . Thought I saw her—could have sworn it was her crossing the street just now—same way—everything—but of course. . . . Of course it wasn't couldn't have been Leon. I know but Christ it was a shock suddenly to see—well to be confronted by someone you've thought dead and. . . . Fancy going out like that honest darling what will people think? Hadn't time—had to see. . . . You're mad really fancy thinking it could have been her when—well when. . . . So like the way she walks you know those long swinging strides turn of the head even the hair. There's a letter from your father Leon he's coming over tomorrow. Oh no. For tea at least we won't go through that performance of his like last time behaves like a child quite unbearable during that film the way he kept belching yawning shouting out he'd got tummy ache hardly saw any of the picture then your step-mother how she panders to him at least his tea won't be sugared and stirred while here why it's almost a working-class habit. He is getting on Ruth I mean eighty-five. He's always been like it those photos as a boy so obviously pampered even then and lapping it up. They moved round each other in the corridor, she clutched the milk bottles, he sank against the wall. A scratching at the door made them look up, at each other. It's the cat oh Leon you left the door open. I don't know—can't remember —I. . . . Ah poor Bobo oh God look he's been bitten look at his poor ear. She passed the bottles to Leonard, and picked the cat up. Quick get something oh dear oh poor Bobos then it's that nasty cat across the way must have got out onto the fire escape somehow. She ran into the bathroom. You're not going to use my flannel Ruth oh God not my flannel please? Shut up it's all your fault you left the door open just look at his poor ear it's all bitten. She dabbed with the flannel, made clucking noises, as the cat lay passive in her arms. Don't like that cat at all bet he attacked the other one first. Of course he didn't Bobo's not vicious in any way. Where's father's letter then? On your desk. He scanned the jerky writing, and tore the letter up. He looked out of the window. The street half empty, the road sweeper shuttled further down, stopped to talk with the park keeper over the railings. Leonard went over to the desk, opened a book, closed it, picked up several books. Think I'll just pop down to the library love. Oh good you can get some shopping then I'll write out a list wonder if we should call the vet Bobo's ear is terribly bitten. He'll be all right Ruth will heal soon enough.

Shopping bag folded under arm, he paused outside the reference library doors, turned away, and walked quickly up the street, across the zebra, through the park gateway. He kept from the main paths filled with women, children, and prams. Took narrow lanes under trees, crossed the wet grass to a small lake, where swans and ducks floated near the edge, they skirted the chairs that had been thrown in, some scattered on the mud, broken, green paint rusty in parts. A faint yellow glow in the sky, cast from the city beyond the water, and trees spread into a darkening greyness as rain slowly drifted in a thin haze, disturbed the smooth surface of the lake. Coat collar turned up, he watched a small boy attempt to capture a toy yacht. His trousers rolled up he tried, with a branch, to bring the boat in, while the boy stood by, clapped his hands and screamed. A gust of wind came up, and the tiny vessel swung round, bobbed out to the middle of the lake. The boy began crying as Leonard struggled back from the mud onto the concrete surround. A woman shouting, ran across the grass towards them. He pulled a scarf from his pocket, flung round his neck, as rain swept across the now deserted park. He sheltered under an oak tree, and watched the toy boat keel over.

Ruth closed the diary, put it back under some papers, books on Leonard's desk. Went over to the chair where the cat, twitching, slept. She looked at his ear, sighed, and stroked him. In Leonard's room she made the bed, picked up a catalogue, gazed at a picture of an orchid, at the numerous forked dark orange-red veins, disc of five yellow raised keels, five short ones on each side, all fringed with crystaline hairs. On another page one with circular rings of dark colour, the base of the complicated lip with two lateral dark purple eyes. She put the catalogue on the bedside table, looked on the ledge underneath, and pulled out pieces of broken statuettes, she held in cupped hands, and tried placing them together, but found they could not be joined for some were missing. She put them back. Closed the window, and watched the women with prams rush from the square to the bus shelter. She moved slowly round the room, picked up various objects, replaced them. She poured some whisky out. In the sitting-room she lit a cigarette, held the match until the flame reached near the end. Put the radio on, switched off, and opened a file of letters, which she thumbed through, picked up another file, and yet another. Opened the desk drawers, groped amongst a pile of paper, pulled out a bundle of letters. A photograph fell face down, she knelt, and turned it over.

He swung out of the park, sheltered in a shop doorway. The street empty of pedestrians, except for an old man bent over from a sandwich board advertising a hearing aid exhibition, who passed up and down the pavement, a muffler covered head, mouth. He was followed by a small dog. Leonard dived out, walked rapidly down the street. In the reference library he spread out some books, pulled up a chair, opposite the old people dozing over magazines.

In the museum section he wandered between the maze of glass cases with stuffed animals, monsters, birds, fish, reptiles. Behind one a couple drew apart as Leonard appeared, and moved behind a larger one, through which he saw the girl's back arched, between butterfly wings, the man's hand passed over her hair, and further down, while she giggled. He passed through galleries, some where students were copying, officials slept in corners. A group of women trouped behind a guide, as Leonard stepped aside, allowing them to pass. A few of the rooms darker than others. In an uncrowded one he sat, stared across at a painting of The Temptation of St. Anthony. He went over, examined it in detail, until the guide's voice behind made him move away, the women's voices, laughter, echoed until he reached the main stairway.

Fumbling for the latch key he rang the bell. God you're soaked darling wipe your feet where in heaven's name have you been and I bet you didn't get those things either? Pouring so hard Ruth I.... But you weren't in the library surely you're soaked through? Went for a walk got caught sorry I didn't get the shopping later perhaps eh love? Nothing in for lunch then your father's coming tomorrow which means we must have some cakes in you know how he guzzles all the time. Been drinking Ruth this early? Just a little warm me up why can you smell it? A little just a little. Leon what's happened to those statuettes you did? Why what made you think of them? Just wondered when I made your bed didn't see them on the table that's all. Broken—yes broken—fell off. But they're in little pieces as though. . . . Oh so you found them? Look as if they've been trodden on or something Leon? Well they weren't much good really. Thought you considered them your best darling? Did I—how's the cat by the way? Looked worse than he actually was think he will be all right that cat of theirs is a monster darling you better change you're wet through God knows what we can have for lunch. Something out of a tin will do Ruth don't worry and we'll go out for dinner o.k.? You going to work this afternoon? Probably—why? Thought we could go to the pictures there's that film. . . . Could put one of our own on Ruth long time since we've done that bring back the memories eh? If you like suppose it'll save us going out in this beastly weather.

In the dark she sat in the middle of the room, while he managed the projector. The screen one side of the white wall. They watched, in silence, at films of themselves with various friends, on the Riviera, looking at landscapes, getting into, out of the car, sitting at cafes, walking down to the sea. Some stills of flowers, orchids, sculpture. A few of the slides upsidedown. Hell something gone wrong— wait a mo—ah that's better. A film of a girl in a bikini, she lay face down on sand. Who's that Leon? Sorry didn't mean to put it on reels got mixed up just a minute I'll change it. No don't I want to look at her. See how she walks Ruth just like the girl I saw this morning. Did she know you were taking it? Can't remember. Strange how she never faces the camera always her head turned away. He switched off. Oh no more? Don't think so. But what's on the rest Leon? Nothing much orchids that's all few of father's sculptures. Any more of us what about the mime play I took darling? Yes should be here somewhere now where is it ah here we are. You look so weird Leon the way you're gesturing it was just before those hooligans came down. Oh God yes look at her movements Ruth how she entered into every part. Yes I guess she had that ability you look so tall Leon behind that grinning mask and the statues look larger too somehow. I think you were a bit out of focus Ruth. There you've taken the mask off suddenly she still has hers on look just look at you doubled up with laughter watching her she's so unaware weaving away amongst those statues oh dear it's running down that's when they must have interrupted any more? No that's the lot just want to put on a still should be here somewhere ah here it is. What's that one called then? It's a Grammatophyllum Scriptum. A what? The Moluccans make a supposedly all-powerful love philtre from its seeds. Really have you any? No wish I had it's a beautiful specimen look at its lip and those veins. It hasn't that foul smell has it like one you have? Ah you mean the Barbigerum. The one I'm thinking about has brown-purple hairs that oscillate when the door opens gives me the creeps ugh well if that's it I'll make the tea. Must get some larger ventilators provide a good sweep of air more easily controllable need some new baskets too must remember to tell the boy not to put the plants so near the window in the summer must be at least a foot from the glass too strong exposure burns the foliage have to keep on repeating instructions to that idiot he's so dense. He packed up the reels, murmuring to himself. Paused over one near the window, letting the end of the film trail on the floor. She clattered with cups, plates. Do move that projector darling what's the one you're looking at now more orchids? Mmmmmmmmm. What a whole film devoted to them? Nodding he rolled the film up. Where shall we go next summer Leon? Don't know love haven't thought about it—where—where would you like? Anywhere as long as we don't go down to Grey House. Well I was thinking of spending some time there want to get the plants out into the garden and see how my hybrids are getting on. A weekend darling not any longer I don't think. . . . A couple of weeks at least Ruth. Then your father will want to come down as well as J—it's all right for you but I have to put up with them more and your step-mother's continual criticisms she's frankly becoming worse too now she's gone all religious. Want to get that wall fixed up also. I'm sure she's bent on converting us in a way I'm glad we haven't a child that would give her more scope for interfering with those snide remarks she makes ugh at least your father doesn't do that though even there he's bullied by her. Have you been tidying my desk Ruth? A bit someone's got to tea's getting cold do come and sit down and stop fluttering around honestly you're like an old woman sometimes Leon. Were you looking in this file? What file darling? He held one up, moved round the table, and faced her. Were you looking for something? Now what would I be spending my time looking through all your paraphernalia for anyway why such questioning have you anything to hide? No—no I just hate things being disturbed you know that. Wish you were more orderly then in your own room don't know what the woman thinks when she does that place. They sat in silence, heads bent over cups.

In the restaurant they sat in a corner reading menus, while the waiter stood behind Leonard. Ruth looked up, fingered her necklace, buttons, attempted to smile at the waiter as Leonard asked for the wine list, over which he took a long time choosing, while the waiter shifted from one foot to the other. Ruth sat back, surveyed the other tables, heads against purple chairs, leaning towards, or away from one another. Men sprawled, asked for cigars, tested, lit by the waiters. Women laughed, smiled demurely, eyes darted round to see who might be glancing their way. Don't look now but right behind you in the other corner I think it's the Murpheys. Really love? He swung round. She pursed her lips, frowning. They've seen us too purposely ignoring us. Imagination Ruth. Well we're certainly not going to acknowledge them after. . . . Oh don't be like that love. He smiled, nodded, raised his glass. How embarrassed she looks and that silly smile of hers really. Ruth raised her glass. And what a ghastly dress she's wearing he's put on weight too just look at her simpering away. She concentrated on her plate. Don't keep looking at them Leon they'll be over before we know where we are. The waiter poured some more wine out. Ruth smiled up, he stepped back, moved smoothly away through the swing doors. That awful laugh of hers so vulgar you wouldn't think she came from a titled family. She leaned back further into the dimly lit alcove. He ate quickly, drained glass after glass of wine, and ordered another bottle. He shifted around, legs moving continually under the table. You know something Ruth I miss having—well when she came out with us she was always so lively good company as they say. But she drank too much that time for instance over the chinese food and vomiting the whole lot up in the ladies such a waste always me who had to cope with it all too. Only once Ruth you do exaggerate. Flirting with everyone waiters included and those long conversations on art you had about which she had no taste at least we re-educated her a bit on paintings oh thank God the Murpheys are going. She nodded, smiled. He went over. She brought out a cigarette, held towards a waiter. She watched Leonard out of the corner of her eyes, laughing, throwing his head back, accepting a cigar.

In the nightclub they watched the floor show. Girls with flesh-coloured tights, sequined bodies, one bent over Leonard, pouted lips, then sprang back. Ruth watched him turn round, clutch his un-lit pipe. The girls shuffled out, and the band struck up a waltz. Do you want to dance Leon? They bumped against each other, couples, in the small ringed off section. This is our tune darling do you remember? What's it called? Oh I can't remember but it's lovely isn't it the first time you invited me out? Mmmmmm. She closed her eyes, head rested against his shoulder. He gazed at the other couples, girls who stared into their partners' eyes, men in bow ties, pressed the available flesh in backless dresses, nuzzled necks, ears. Small men with tall girls, jerked backwards, forwards. The spotlight fell on bald heads. Waiters leaned against pillars. The music merged into a faster rhythm. Couples sprang apart, twisted away, back again. Leonard swung from side to side, while Ruth flung her arms out, head rotated quickly. Sit this one out I think love. Ohhhhh no Leon it's lovely look I can do it just watch. She flung herself back, shoulders twitching, hands shook around her body, his. He moved slowly from the hips, on the one spot, as she flung herself round faster and faster, a look of concentration on her face. He focused upon a smudge of lipstick on her chin. Her mouth open, eyes closed, hair came undone, she continued dancing, even when the band stopped. Breathing rapidly she approached Leonard in swaying movements. It's great—hold me—hold me—hold. . . . He took her hand and pulled her back to their table. She collapsed, adjusted a brassiere strap, tidied her hair. Her hand shook as she held a cigarette out for him to light. What about some more to drink darling? I think you've had enough Ruth really you know you suffer in the morning if . . . Oh just a small one a brandy come on? She breathed over the glass, tapped her feet, eyes closed, she smiled. Just like that first evening except of course then I was so shy and nervous. He lit his pipe, and sank back, tilting the chair, he watched the girls come on, behind huge fans, which they swung away, back again over their half naked bodies. And I fell asleep do you remember Leon and you carried me out of the car? She giggled, opened her eyes, picked her glass up, she watched him lean forward, loosen his tie. She touched an artificial flower. Not really very good are they awful legs some of them have. Oh I don't know Ruth better than at that other place. The band struck up a finale. The girls came forward, bent their heads, and swept off their wigs. People applauded loudly, cheered. Ruth collapsed laughing. Well I'm damned all bloody men who would have thought it fantastic quite fantastic. Imagine going off with one of those Leon hahahahahahahahahahah poor old thing do you feel cheated then —ohhhhhhhhhhhhhh dear ohhhhhhhh how funny you look. The men wriggled off, holding their wigs, fans aloft. She blew smoke rings into the flowers.

In the car the radio blared. Rain slashed the roof, windows, as they swung through winding, wet streets. She wrapped a rug round her legs, closed her eyes. Wake up love hey wakey up we're here. Mmmmmmm—oh Leon you know I'm more tight than I realised oh dear oops. He helped her as she stumbled across the pavement, held the revolving doors. The hall porter in his doorway, said goodnight, opened the lift gates. In the corridor she leaned against the wall, giggling, tears streamed over her cheeks, making blotches in the powder. Oh dear I can't get over those girls turning out and you there you were you ohhhhhhh dear ohhhhhhhh. Like some coffee Ruth? Ohhhhhhhhh. He opened her door, lifted her onto the bed, where she lay, her dress above her thighs. At the end of the bed, he looked down. She opened her eyes suddenly. Why you staring at me like that darling what's the matter? Thought you asieep want some coffee? Be nice. Pulling her dress down, she looked in the mirror. Oh God what a mess I am oh dear oh Christ. She lay back, hand covered the mirror.

He sat on the edge of the bed, gazed into his cup. Leon do you have fantasies when—well when we make love ever I mean do you love? Just wondered not obscene things darling not awful dirty things like—like. . . . Depends on how you think on these matters. What sort of fantasies Leon? Oh I don't know depends. . . . Depends on what? Mood I suppose. Who do you think of—who—when you. . . . Oh not a particular person Ruth what about yourself? Oh never I mean it's always you just you I mean women aren't supposed to are they apart from images of their lover or something like that but tell me what you think Leon when we make love go on do tell Ruthy won't you will you won't you? She crawled across the bed, held her face close, under his. He stroked her nose, plucked her lips. Can't really can't recall any at the moment. She did Leon awful things or at least whoever she made love with did sort of verbal fantasies I suppose some people have to a kind of compensation I think. Mmmmm what would you do if I did that you know started saying things? Such as what Leon? She held away from him, looked at her rings, which she pulled off. I want to fuck you? Oh Leon don't use that word it's so awful. As good a word as any—it's—well it's immediate as she would have said. Well I don't like it. She heaved her dress off. He lay back and looked at the ceiling. Undo me will you please darling? He knelt on the bed, unhooked her brassiere, his hands round her, lifted her breasts up. Turning she leaned over him. Look like dancing. He watched her wriggle above. Catching a breast he began sucking, clutched the other, he looked at her face contort, flushed, wrinkled. She attempted to struggle away. Laughing he brought his legs round her, pressed against her thighs. Her head swung, until hair fell over his face. What you thinking now Leon? Nothing love just feeling and you? That you look like a baby doing this. That's all I am mmmmmm oh ah. He gurgled, sucked, clutched harder. Ah don't darling you're hurting you're bruising me you know how tender I am. She pulled back. Look you've made me bleed oh really Leon why do you do it? Rigid, he mouthed the pillow. Just like the cat. . . . What was that—what did you say Leon? Nothing—nothing. Oh I'm tired so tired. She stepped out of the rest of her clothes, moved heavily over to the dressing-table. I knew you'd bruised me just look nasty purple marks all over. She faced the bed. Groaning, he turned over onto his stomach. Sometimes you're like a beast Leon the way you. . . . Well get yourself someone else Ruth a nice sweet tender gentle little boy. How can you say that really Leon? She pulled on her nightdress. Oh damn run out of cigarettes have you any darling? No I haven't. Not even any of those French ones left? No. You couldn't be a poppet and go to the machine round the corner? O.k. o.k. Put your coat on darling you'll catch cold and don't forget the door we don't want Bobo to get out again got your keys?

He shrank in the doorway as some drunks shouting crossed the road, arms round one another. He waited until they had disappeared, until their laughter grew faint, before stepping out, slowly down the street. A woman at the bus stop said hello lovey coming home with me tonight? He shook his head. She shrugged and walked to the bus shelter across the road. He shoved the coin into the machine which he banged and kicked. Nothing happened. He crouched over, the rain sliding down his face.

She smoothed some cream onto her cheeks, nose, and neck,

brushed out her hair. She put on the radio and danced in front of the mirror. Hearing laughter she went to the window. A light on in the opposite building, a man stood there, smiling, he waved. She shivered, drew the curtains, and faced the room, hand curled tight against herself.

He walked near the park railings. Over-hanging branches dripped. Beacon lights flashed on empty roads, reflected. Sound of rain on pavements, and his heavy tread back, hands in pockets. The porter's dog whined, thudded against the door. Whirring of lift, humming as it slowed down. He tapped on Ruth's door, opened a little, then closed. Quietly he set the projector up, and put a film on. A girl, naked, emerged from the sea, hair over her face, she approached, then turned away. Picked up a towel, held out to the wind. Her back straight, toes curled in the sand. Ridges of sand, corrugated near the breakwater, where she leaned, the towel wrapped round her. In slow motion gulls circled as she approached again, towel clutched round half her body, a mask covered her face. She danced away to the edge of the sea, where she flung towel and mask down, dived into a huge wave, bobbed up, hair and seaweed caught in spray. The film slowed down. He stared at the square piece of light on the wall, in the middle flecks of black like hair. He switched off. In the dark he sat, hands over his face.

    Sound of sea.
Waterfall
trees
in the wind.
Traffic
at night.
A pool
to bathe in.
Humid nights. Naked
under a sheet. Making faces out of branches.
Faces known
unknown. One taking over
another. Hallucinations
falling.
Apples. Half eaten into.
Hooded
skulls
nod. Hands beckon. Voices call
from mouths
that do not open. Eyes broken
into
shredded
layers of grey tissue take on forms. Move in circles.
Rain
on water.

The single buzzing of a bluebottle
banging
into its own shadow. A crab climbed onto a stick
swayed
fell off. Scurried towards a rock. Their shadows made it change
course. Slant back. He crushed it. She ran screaming towards the
cliff. He pounded after her. Sideways.
A bear
on hind legs. To the call of gulls. Sandcastles
effigies
fortresses. Legs apart as the tide came in. Days of sun
then
in grass.
On snow
the ridges. Rolled over. Down the hill where
trees always waited. Held secrets.
Secrets
of days spent away from school.
Pine cones
towers
acorns. For eyes. Leaves for a dress. The village church entered
only at harvest time. Stained glass
light
flowers
leaned towards. Musty
smell of
dry leaves. A dampness. In that half darkness.
Graves with
over-grown moss. Wild flowers
sheltered from the wind. Crept
over the hill.
He loves me he loves me
not
loves
me
not
yes

no. No? Blades of grass
fall
through fingers. Necklaces re-strung. And the light from
a buttercup
held
under the chin. His jutting out. Hers
tucked in. Movements coloured
now. Pebbles in water
take out
regard. As the first time seeing stars. Walking the
endless
unlit Gap. Her tears
held back. He disappearing in the theatre. Just an argument dear
your father was a bit upset I really don't know why. Expanse of
sky
her cold hand. His pounded the door in the morning.
Reconciliation. Later cups thrown through the bead curtain.
Their shouts.
Hiding under
the grand piano. Friends called over the broken gate that finally
collapsed as Aunt Polly's coffin passed out.
Her black velvet dress put in the trunk.
The smell
of her
of oranges peeled. In the room
handed over
at the top of the house. Where a bird fell
down the chimney. The wind
imprisoned. A last scream from Grandma Alice. Her room
of stale cakes
medicine. The ornamental chamber pot with the crack half way
down
later as a salad bowl used.
Jam made in a saucepan. I've never had a proper preserving pan.
She said. Carefully writing dates on jars. Most treasured possession
a pair of kid gloves. Her mother saved up for. The oath they swore
to the Band of Hope and Glory.

For life
to go on picnics. Wearing
Sunday best. Their mother made. Though we were poor no one
ever knew. But how we envied the girls in fur coats who came
out of the ammunition factories. They dressed in rags before the
war. We lived on mackerel father caught that's why I can't eat
fish now. Her cheeks flushed
by the fire
remembering. And the lovely wax doll put by the fire that melted.
I don't know if my sister did it intentionally she was always for
some reason a bit jealous of me I think . . . poked fun at my red
hair funny she should dye hers later the same colour and the
sapphire ring she stole I wondered why she insisted on buying me
a present the day I couldn't find it.
Blue flowers
cowslips
on the downs. Larks became specks.
Their nests
never found.

Dreams of horses
corpses
the house
at the top of the avenue. Added dimensions. The room
when the grand piano was taken away.
The stool
Auntie Marmee made higher. Playing the only tune she knew.
By ear.
The Blue Danube. Over
and over
again. Senile at seventy. Calling for her nephew. Who never
came. Money she saved put in a box
for him
when he was not touring. Why I never made it dear was because

—well honestly because they could never make up their minds whether I was a baritone or bass-baritone. What roles did he play then? Oh he never got beyond the chorus. She said. Though there were concerts arranged at the Hall. But his father even had to finance those. So he started up businesses. That failed. An optician's. He was an optician you know when you were born. Forever falling in love with pianists. Twice his age. Prima Donnas. Who thought they were. The one who was fond of cats. A dozen on the bed. It's them or me. He said. Jumping off. The trouble was I always took him back every time he was unfaithful. So full of repentance what could I do? Yet so jealous of me if I ever looked at another man. It was a very physical relationship between your mother and myself really—ah yes she was lovely—lovely in those days still is I suppose but I wanted—what did I want? Someone who shared everything you know a real artist complete understanding freedom yes independence and all that. We sat by a fountain. He made noises to the pigeons. Told funny stories of places. Digs in the provinces. Jokes in the company. You know A Masked Ball dear well we called it A Masked Testicle. His eyes folded. Then there's a line the chorus had and instead of singing consternation we said constipation—yes really constipation—we had oh yes we had great fun in those days. Where's he working now then? What on earth is he doing in the Foreign Office? No no couldn't stick it dear even though it might have meant a good pension not worth it really well I'm doing a postal course in chiropody work at it every evening won't be long now before I graduate as it were and can set up a place somewhere nice a resort perhaps there's quite an income really in it you know nowadays. Ha-ha-ha
you and me
little brown jug
how I love thee
singing. Auntie Marmee skipped. Hopped. In the kitchen. Bead curtains parted. Your father's coming home tomorrow I'll make a nice bread pudding he likes my bread puddings. Your Aunt was never a good cook but she made marvellous bread puddings all the lovely sugar on top now even I couldn't make them as nice

as that. Of course she doted on your father. And when he left
she pressed an envelope that jingled in his hands. Never forget
my dear no matter what happens he is after all your own father.
Leaves fell
wind
howled
under the back door. Bills
piled up
on the chest of drawers. Top shelf.
The pipes
froze. Run down dear and call the plumber up oh God when shall
we ever have a winter without the pipes bursting?
She said coming back from the chemists. Where she worked.
Smelling of sulphur. Coughing the first signs
of bronchitis. And over the hill the village pond might have ice
in the night.
Thick enough
to walk across
avoid those
who had
skates
ponies. And exchanged visits
on Sundays. Who had
boyfriends
partners
at the dances. In the Public Hall. Clutching high heels
in carrier bag. White dresses.
Waiting
wondering why.
Longing
for a Paul Jones
Ladies' Excuse Me. Being dared. Not daring. Stealing out before
the last waltz. Across
the downs
without shoes. Dancing a wild
dance. A solo orgy there
in the dew pond. Round the windmill. Summoning the four

winds to
ride through the stars. Lift off
the crust
of the world below. Seven seas of green contained
there
where ghosts and God were confided in
argued with. Questioned as clouds pressed closer.
Separated
formed arcs. Raced the sea to the moon. Grass heavy
with dew.
A heaviness of earth. Shadows. Before the village
clock
struck. Midnight. Were you the belle of the ball darling then?
Oh dear well never mind they're not such a nice crowd down
there what a shame though you looking so pretty in that dress I
made you didn't you even have one dance? Perhaps you don't
smile enough dear? I hope you came back with the others? Her
hair in curlers. Smelling of warm sheets and oven. She closed a
book. Arms out for the goodnight kiss. I've put a hot-water bottle
in for you and if you're hungry there's some cookies in the cake
tin but don't eat them all there's a good girl.
To the house. Where the balcony hangs half way. Suspended.
Above
the overgrown garden. She wonders why the tomatoes she looks
at every day never go beyond being green or yellow. Rows of
sweetpeas tied to canes. Struggle through weeds. Wild roses
scattered
against
the broken outhouse wall. And the neighbour across the way.
Whose wife died yesterday. Or the day before. Of an internal
growth. Who's deaf. Has a pianola. He draws steam ships.
Writes vast manuscripts in hieroglyphics. Said to be dictated by
an Egyptian princess. The British Museum quite interested. Books
he scribbled in every day. Throughout the night. Published at his
own expense. Talks of reincarnation. Cries if a spider's killed.
That may have been a relative. Turns his deaf aid off. When
creditors call. Sealed the bedroom door. After his wife died.

Nibbles lettuce leaves all day Sunday. Lets the children pedal out
old fashioned tunes. Shakes his fists at those. Who steal
his apples
play in his field
full of mole-hills. Died in his attic. Amongst books.
Lay
stiff
for a week. So they said. Poor old Hume. And Mr. Hogg.
A distant cousin. Who came to stay. For a weekend. Stayed for
a month. Smelling.
of brandy
tobacco
dirty underwear.
Broken veins
on face. Had the D.T's. When no one was looking. Fondled
children. On his
knees. Told tales
of distant days. When singers were singers. And whisky
nearly as cheap as bread. Sang
three old ladies
locked in a lavatory. To his own tune. Struggled with his shadow
on the landing walls
Poor old Hogg
He's nothing but a dog
Pulled the plug
Thought it was a bug
Borrowed some money. Was never seen again.
Concerts arranged on Saturday nights. After the table tapping.
An upturned glass round an unframed mirror.
Relatives. And pets
from the other side
spelt out strange words. Everyone whispered about. For days
after. In dreams
Auntie Marmee entered
the room
at the top of the house. With dog's head. And paws tapped.
The end of the bed. Barked as she wriggled up the chimney.

Leaving behind
a portrait
of her nephew. All yellow. Wrinkled. Dressed in sailor suit.
While Grandma Alice
hung
on the door. Without legs. Breathing asthmatic tales of treachery.
Complained the tea was cold. Banged her spittoon against Aunt
Polly's head. Whose hair trailed into insect sperm. Ringed fingers
groped
under
the large stone. Amongst an ants' nest. In the corner of the room.
The silver teapot. China cups. Brought out. On Sunday afternoons. Her hands
still with faint traces of flour. Passed scones around. After they
had clapped politely. He pigeon chested. Collapsed in leather arm-
chair. Where cushions hid the torn parts. She sat beside the
Japanese table. Inlaid with ivory. At one time. Laid her little
finger over the cup. She'd stuck together. With glue. While the
children upstairs peed in tiny cups. For the dolls' tea party. Painted
each other's private parts. Dared the eldest to show what were
still growing. You mustn't play with yourself down there dear you
might injure yourself and regret it when you're older. She said.
And why was Tommy crying when he left? Aren't you friends
with Jo then any more? For heaven's sake don't go out and play
in your new coat I bought that for you to wear as best it cost a
fortune there's your siren suit I made you for playing in. The zip
that went all the way up.
And down.
The others laughed at. Except when the snow came. They were
pushed down the hill. Into the nettles.
The downs. Behind.
held hollows. Fists. Clusters of trees. A sea of grass.
Changed with the movement of clouds. The sun
edged
over. By some mysterious power. Transformed
glass
into water. Birds shook icicles from their feathers.

99

Scarecrows became scarecrows again. And he went on tour once more. Up North. Letters became fewer. Until
the one
she had been
waiting for
finally came. Which she read. Put away. And read again.
If only she'd have made more of a scene well I. . . .
What could I do dear but give him his freedom perhaps I thought he'd come back he'd done it after all so often before.

A change over-night almost desired. As when waking from a dream
and going back. But it alters of itself. I always believe that no matter what happens it is for the best. As one door shuts another opens that's my philosophy always has been. She'd say. Attempting to cover the blood clot with powder, lipstick. On her upper lip. Ah well that's life and things must go on. Perhaps it's for the best. She'd murmur. Over addings up. In margins of the newspaper. And walk two streets away if tea was tuppence cheaper there.
Stand for hours at an auction. Buy
Windsor chairs
strange antiques. Usually the colour of blue. Make do
with broken spectacles
teeth
slippers
and weird wiring. That made men wince. Draught proof strips. Cut out of lino. That's the worst of a woman on her own. She'd say. Putting towels near the door. To keep the wind out. Shyly protective over plants. I must be greenfingered you know no one else can make them grow like that. Busy Lizzies crowded the sills. Plants flowered. That weren't meant to flower. She had forgotten the names of. Dresses she made for herself. Do you know dear they couldn't believe I'd made it myself and all by hand too.

On hands and knees round the floor. Placing pattern pieces on material. Pins in her mouth. Oblivious. Wish I had a nice large table to do it on. A proper preserving pan. And copper pots like they have next door. She bends over the brass box. With the scene of the den of thieves. That stores coal. Gently rubs the remaining liqueur glasses. Out of a set of twelve. Plates with paintings on. In the glass cabinet. Brightly coloured cushions. She had also made. By hand. What we really need now is a nice settee get rid of all these old chairs. She'd wistfully sigh. Twist the imitation sapphire ring. Light another cigarette. Worry about what next to do. What had not been done. What there was to do. What might happen. In two weeks' time. That never happens.
Tells of strange dreams
she remembers
after they have come true. Eats
bunches
of watercress. Swears it stops the pins and needles in her arm. Broken when a child. Bears in a plate of crumpets.
Contained
in a quiet excitement. Draws up her chair. Closer to the fire. Begins to knit another mohair jumper. Plans a sailing holiday. A cruise. Trips to the islands. Never going further than the travel brochures. So much to do dear in the flat then there's the plants who would look after those?

A place that becomes
another place. Defeats time. Contradicts
movements
gives dimensions. As on a hill
seeing
the very field only the day before
appeared
to be a vast jungle. Irony. They do not comprehend in
each other.

From themselves. He shuts himself off in a room to work.
Bringing the tea in. The bed is ruffled. His hair stands up. Paper
scattered.
on desk
floor. She sits in front
of the mirror
for hours. In an afternoon
sighs
combs the fringe carefully over lines on her forehead.
Does exercises every morning. Except when the weather is too hot
too cold. Go for picnics in the car. Laughing
chattering
on the way. Returning in silence. What thoughts possess them?
While waiting at a railway crossing. At dusk. Sound of rain
beginning. The train
listened for.
Then there. Emerging from the tunnel. Glimpse of white faces
frozen
against windows. She strains back. He leans forward. Rubs the
windscreen. Lights for a moment. Show up their faces. Eyes.
Her eyes of someone shocked.
Interrupted
but from what?
Habits they parcel up
hand to each other. As if marked not to be opened until the day.
Breakfast at eight
Lunch at one
Tea at four
Dinner at seven
The cat fed three times. A day. Titbits in between. But not if
he's killed a bird. Stray cats. Dogs yelled at. Pushed out. The
house tidied up before. After. The cleaner comes. Days
hours
spent. Clearing the mess. Trespassers make. Orchids. The pots.
Broken. Difficult to tell whether a storm had been the cause. Or
not. He swears. Grumbles. As he re-pots. Under trees. Discusses
further how to effect pollination. The little yellow or whitish

pieces are placed so on the surface of the stigma of the female parent. All orchidaceous plants are hybridised in this fashion. Pollinated flower should enlarge within a few days. He anxiously waits. Shows a three inch egg-shaped one. Narrowed below into a stalk
heavy-textured. Flowers of waxy texture. With a heady fragrance. She draws back from. He breathes softly into. Touches the yellow red-marked lips. The front magenta-red.
Thin-textured leaves. Formed into a loose fan. Blotched red-brown. Lip small. Yellow-marked. Cylindrical. And he talks of moderate applications of fertiliser. Abundant moisture light.
The lightning. She shrinks away from. Refuses to have the television on. In case the house should be struck. They sit in candle-light. Waiting for the rumble of thunder.
Released
from the mountains. She stalks the house. With the cat. Draws all the curtains. Jumps out of her chair. What was that? Just another statue fallen. Perhaps. Then they came. In the middle of a storm. One night. Waving torches.
Throwing
fireworks
into the swimming pool. Stampeded
round the statues. While he stood quivering. In the summer-house. In the dark. They screamed. Tore flowers out. She buried her face in cushions. Crying. Hands covered her ears. Then they left. When the storm passed. A trail of torn flowers left. Plants. Broken bronze pieces.
Littered paths.
Over lawns.
In the empty swimming pool a balloon floated. Oblong. Yellow. That bumped. But did not burst. Against the sides.

The lake
in the middle
of the mountains. Isn't marked on the map. We'll go up there
perhaps tomorrow. They say. Oh dear it would rain. She says.
Going back to play patience. He with orchids. Manipulates the
spray. Densely spotted ones.
Arranged in
longitudinal rows
confluent. Petals sharply
deflected
downwards
short
orange hairs. He touches. With little finger. And talks
of the operation in cross-pollination. Showing a flattened tooth-
pick. He uses. Palm of his hand
held
under the column. You see when the stigma is mature and ready
for fertilisation—look can you—come nearer look see how sticky
and moist it is to touch.
In the sand
dunes
our fingers
touched. Accidentally. He sat up. And smoked. The
sand
slid into
grass above. Suppose it's time to go back. The shouts of those
behind the breakwater. Their laughter
sound of transistors
bonfires
at night.
Fireworks. Remains of rockets
in the swimming pool. Eye sockets. His blood. After they came
down. Hurled themselves. Pieces of metal at him. A glove.
Handed over to the police. Never identified. He swathed in
bandages. On mid-summer's day.
A window of the summerhouse broken. If they get at my orchids
again I'll murder them curse them why do they do it why why why?

She sits
at the piano
looks out of the window. Hours
of patiently
waiting.
Days
of impatience. Let's have a cup of tea. Shall we play pontoon?
Chinese Rummy? Consequences? Where are the masks? Let's
pretend we're the only inhabitants left after an atomic war. Or
prisoners all in one cell. Chairs mark the boundary line. She
stepped over saying I can't go on. While he knocked invisible
walls
pushed against
bars. Not there. Sat
and played
with a piece of invisible string. Hung himself with it.
Windows open
a breeze
stirs
the curtains. A mouse on the terrace steps. He picked up with a
garden rake. Before she came down. For breakfast.
Torn lizards. Skins
shiny
in the flowerbeds. The ruby one she wears on an evening dress.
Pauses in the doorway. Approves guests. Waits for their approval.
The sweep
rustle
of long dresses
on the terrace. At weekends. The trail of those. Round statues
Emptying ash-trays. Glasses
bottles
in the morning. Gossip repeated. Extended. Friends
of friends. Stayed on for breakfast
lunch
dinner. The slamming of car doors. Waving out of windows.
She goes back to the piano. Hands folded. Only for a moment
in that silence. While he carefully unpacked orchids from abroad.

Marked ' Books '. To evade the customs. Health authorities.

In the evenings rowing out
towards
the mountains. Mid-way. Oars rested.
Dipped
in clear water
green. Fish lying
motionless
at the bottom. Mountain peaks
cut off
by clouds. The one that will be climbed soon
Soon.
One can get lost up there if a mist comes suddenly down you
might easily fall. They say. Someone drowned in the lake that
way. Sun
absorbed
sinks
behind the purple. Spreading. Porcupine quills
across the water. Sound
of oars
creaking. Of boat. Jumping onto the shore. Resting on the edge.
As fishing boats are pushed out.
Behind
the breakwater
a few stragglers
pack up their belongings. In plastic bags. Catch the last bus back.
To the holiday camp. Deck chairs left to reserve their territory
for the next day. Made into shelters when the rain. And wind
come. The ice cream man. A plumber during the winter. Counts
out his takings on a rock.

Lying in the sun
on the terrace. The beach. They sip iced drinks. Rub each other's
backs. Legs. He shouts from the breakwater. Meet under water.
Fall
into reveries. The bed an ocean
down
up
over. Hanging above. Hold me there. Spray in the mouth.
Dilated eyes. Those in their glass houses at the zoo. Asleep—
dead? Tiny pulses beat. Could be electronically done. A python
curled about itself. Behind a white rabbit
dead. A man in mac contemplates donkeys. An old woman. In
grey. Bends over railings. Wonders at a lump of
African mammal. Lions
heard
roaring. But not seen. Chimpanzees stare. Crouch on a single
bar. Scratch behind glass. Camels urinate. Sealions play with
fish. Gulls gather
there
from the river.
Here. Their moans at night. Rest on statues. Waiting.
For the crumbs
she might throw out.

On the terrace
warmer nights. Dinner. Music drifts through open doors.
Stars
fall
away. And the sea sometimes heard. But hardly seen. He leans
against the wall. Sighs with after dinner satisfaction.
Sometimes quotes a poem. In German. Italian. She fetches her
knitting. But hands
idle
she stares

into the garden. Shivers. And goes inside. The light from her
bedroom slants down
on the terrace walls. He winds his watch. Knocks pipe against
his shoe. Contemplates ice in glass. The scent of lilac. Perfume.
She rubbed behind ears. Wrists. Contours of his face. In the half
light. Shirt unbuttoned. At the neck. Where the pulse must
beat. He talks. But more to himself. If left he'd hardly notice.
Yet be puzzled when realising he was on his own. Facing the
whisky bottle. Returning from a swim
breathless
warm
wet
laughing
for no reason. Other than from
a sense of conspiracy. A moon madness. On the back.
Sting
of water
smell of it in lungs. Globular parts. Of white flesh.
Circles
of darkness. Was it cold then? He'd pour out a drink. Lean
across the table. As though he'd breathe in the after-effects of
well-being. Without attempting to experience
the sea
at night. Daytime his white legs. Arms. Stems broken off suddenly. By a combine. As a breaker heaved over. Sometimes he
dived into one. Rose. Shaking his head. Hair in thin streaks over
eyes. He parted. To see if anyone had been watching. She remained stretched out. A sandy part.
Sheltered
by rocks. Slipped her bathing costume down. Only when turning
over. On her stomach. Shook the sand out of her hair. From her
hands. Made hollows
in the sand
With her feet
legs. Their veins the skin of fruit.
Surrounded by
hats

towels
wraps
basket. She hands out the food
ceremoniously. While he peels pears
apples
oranges. Buries the skins carefully. Reads without turning a page.
Until she asks for her back to be rubbed. He turns the page over
quickly. Murmuring. His fingers in the hollow of back. Dig
smooth over.
Aware of her breath. Cloves. And the imprint of bodies.
Afterwards.
Footprints
of others
in the morning. A dead gull. Wings spanned. Head to one side.
She shuddered at. He threw into the sea. White bones of fish.
Ivory-smooth. In solitary places. Away from the bunches
of seaweed.
sucking noises of shells. After the tide goes out. Screams from
children. The other side. Shouts of the ice cream man.
Flapping deckchair canvas
flags.
Orange peel
newspaper. Tossed over.
Paper bags. Black patches up near the grass.
Between
sand dunes. Where bonfires have been. He stares at as though at
some skin disease. He knows the cause of. But not the cure. He
heaps sand over. Makes plans for putting up more notices.
A wall
traps
burglar alarms. Getting an Alsatian dog. In the garden. The
swimming pool only a breeze disturbs.
Poplar trees erect as Greek columns. Bring attention to the sky.
Silent wheeling of gulls. Flurry of swallows. A few small clouds.
Disperse. Before reaching the other side of the mountains.
The other side. A flat landscape of marsh. Carrion wait on dead
tree stumps

branches
limp arms
hang.   Roads lead nowhere.   Mosquitoes whir continuously.
Where water sucks in the sun.   The land a floating mass of vegetation. Limbs of trees
embedded
congealed mud. With particles of leaves
feathers
fur. High shrieks of an animal. Bird. Unseen. Followed by a
heavy silence.   Again.   Echoed by the mountains.   In the pass.
A tunnel made from surrounding rock.   Emerging to see the lake.
As if held in cupped hands.   A piece of glass.   Easily trodden on.
From that distance.   But it's many miles long.   They say.   Opening the car windows. But not getting out. Behind. Tufts of grass.
Flowers.   Crawl from rocks.   Sheep pause.   Stare.   Fall over each
other into the valley.

Hours
perhaps just minutes.   By the waterfall
on the breakwater
sand
at night.   Dancing.   Tempting the moon to show.   Warmth still.
Of sun
on rocks
long after sunset.   The lights from fishing boats.   A
chain
of lights as though on their own.   In line
dividing.   Collision of water
rocks
bodies
hands. Demanding more. From the night than they would dare
to by day. Sharing a cigarette. The contact it promises.
Fall
of rain

sheltering in a cave
against the wall. Heavy breathing. Thud of rain
footsteps that might be there.
Exposed
to a world. Laughed at
in apprehension. Taste of salt. Slithering into
other caves. As through grass. Behind the house. Beyond the
avenue
on the downs. Where the moon
climbed slowly
became bigger than the world. Would surely break
split
into a thousand pieces. Yet aware of other worlds floating.
Disintegrated. Leaving gaps
as sleep. In an afternoon. The whole of a dream. Comprehended.
Parts lost like stolen flowers dropped on the way back.

Back in the city. A heatwave. It can't last. Everyone exclaimed.
Parks filled. Half naked bodies. Men worked in offices
without jackets. Windows in the flat
all open. A fan whirred day and night
night and day. She lay on the sofa in the afternoons.
Chain-smoked
drank long cool drinks. He walked
through the park
quickly. Eyes
on the path ahead.
Girls' laughter. Their skirts above bare knees. Men with shirt
sleeves rolled up. Traffic moves languidly. People wave from
open cars. Going to the sea resorts. Or just returning. She looks
through countless magazines. Washes hair every other day.
Bought various powders for the cat who has tapeworms. Who
vomits everything up in corners
of the room.

On his bedspread. He threw the cat into the corridor.
She screamed
threw books at him. That knocked a painting off the wall. He
was called away. Abroad for a week. Suddenly. She went to the
hairdressers. Bought several dresses. Hats.
Went out for
tea
lunch. Invited friends round for dinner. And went to the pictures.
Or theatre. For four days. The fifth day she stayed in bed. Curtains drawn. Radio on. Just have a bad period. She said. Oh
are you going out? Do stay with me. An orange light
interior of some exotic flower
hovered
over walls. Smell of heavy perfume.
Bodies. Hers. Only the shape moulded from the sheet. Will you
brush my hair?
Long
thick
over shoulders. Stay with me a little longer it's early yet. In that
yellow enclosure
sipping
whisky and ice. He hasn't even sent a card this time I hope he's
all right. She rushed to the letterbox every morning. Wish we'd
stayed in the country oh God it's so dull so boring here so hot if
only it would change something would happen if only. . . .
Then he returned. A day early. Loaded
with parcels.
Standing in the doorway
flushed
trying to bend. For his welcome. The parcels slipped from his
arms. She picked up
laughing
untied. But what on earth are they? Robes to wear for miming.
Oh is that all. She said
lifting
three identical white robes
out of their boxes. Anything else?

A lovely book on the Renaissance and a jolly good one on fertilisation. Orchids of course—what did you think?

The furniture re-arranged. A game played. She refused to wear
her robe. The wrong size. Committed to strange manoeuvres
comprehended by him
in moments. When he stopped laughing. Adjusted his mask.
In the heat. Robes clinging. As a weekend
in a hotel
room. Meals brought up. And not eating.
Avoiding
the issue
possibility. For the last time. Remembering only the first. Climbing the stairs
knowing
the receptionist looked.
Two days
nights
spent in
over. The bed. Heavy curtains threw off
a thin light. Shreds of street lighting. Talking of other affairs
parts played. Believed
made to believe in. The loneliness
of sun
coming up
over the sea. Lap
lapping. Slap
of water. Sand too hot
for the naked foot. Compelled to talk
about everything. Except what there was
to be confronted by. Talk
turned in upon itself. Dried stains on sheets.
Apple cores
in ash trays. The dot of cigarette light. Before pretence

at sleep.
Waiting
for that
first faint light. In a darkened room. Hurt me hurt
me hurt me
there
here
anywhere. This way. If you like. Talk to me talk.
Talk
to
me
Was it like this with
Never before. Not like this. No one has touched me ever
never never
like this. Before. Like waves. The coming
slowly. Dual roles
realised. Yes yes
yes
Be a boy. If you like. Anything. Be
Just be

The hot spell continued. Parks over-flowed. Let's get back.
Breathe. They said. By the sea
again.
The other side. Invalids. Came down
on crutches. Left by the breakwater. They crawled on stomachs.
Into
the water. Early mornings. Old men
in white
reared
whiter heads. Faces. Whose eyes were failing.
Blue
purple veined hands. Lifted
to the sun. As they squatted in pools. Or helped those who had

no hands.
No legs.
No arms. Some blind
held their heads
higher
laughed louder. Threw down their sticks
against rocks.
In the garden. Poplar trees
rigid
spaced out. The sky.
The waterfall
trickled. And everything
waited. Stopped waiting
adapted. Then the change came. In the change. The knowledge
of what had to be done
what there is
to do. As the leaves
changed colour. The air
sharper. Signs
of frost
watched for. Days become shorter. Hours lengthen. Wind rises
out of the sea
carries mist
to the house. Buries itself
into stonework. The possibility of what might have been sinks
away. Into what is left.

Leonard pressed the switch down, and looked across at Ruth. No more then? That's the lot only two reels. And not a word not a clue. Why did you expect something love? I wondered who . . . She bit her lip as he banged down the lid. Who what Ruth? Oh nothing except perhaps I thought she might have talked about suicide given us something definite but there's nothing absolutely nothing there maybe the journals yes perhaps there . . . Most suicides do it on the spur of the moment anyway without much thought. That's a fallacy Leon if ever there was there are some people who write notes saying they've been contemplating it for forty years. Oh who doesn't think about it. Why do you darling? He stared at the tape. Maybe. What do you mean maybe? Well makes life that much more of a miracle perhaps no not really Ruth no need to worry you won't be a widow yet I'll await my turn. She looked up at him, frowning. Sometimes I don't understand you at all almost as if there's another side to you. Ahhhhhh hidden depths eh Ruth? She certainly had what did she want of us Leon what was she after I really don't understand unless . . . Yes? She was a little in love with you in a strange way and who—who . . . In love with love I think Ruth plus a father complex. Ugh that man honestly how anyone could have put up with him. He shrugged, lifted the recorder off the table. And pity her poor mother. Oh he doesn't sound that bad Ruth a sort of sad failure perhaps he's the more to be pitied. Strange how she never says who she was involved with. Did she never tell you Ruth you know how women . . . Never I had a feeling though she was involved at one time with someone married but . . . Oh probably had several. Yet she talks writes as if only the one . . . Remember that freak weather in the summer Ruth days and days of it trouble is we're just not used to the sun in this country. I suppose she was rather sensual did you find her sexy Leon? Certainly had a way of moving well. You were never attracted by her ever Leon? What's this an interrogation she was a child Ruth besides I—I . . . Yes? She leaned over, towards him, away. Well you were saying? Let's face it neither of us understood her there was a need in her for security yet at the same time she rebelled background convent family everything contributed . . . I always felt you understood her Leon more than I ever could. Perhaps—perhaps and yet . . . Funny how she observed us quite honestly I would never have recognised ourselves from her descriptions. Aspects only aspects Ruth cold then love? No. You were shivering I thought . . . Let's go in the other room far cosier. Let's go out. Where? Anywhere this flat oh I don't know. You're always so restless Leon. He bowed over the desk, looked at a painting and straightened it. Where can we go I thought I'd wash my hair? The park? It's so cold. A brisk walk Ruth do you good. I'm tired you go I have a bit of headache too. Sighing, she rested her head against the chair. He stared at her until she looked up. Think I'll just pop out a little while get some air in my lungs. Put something warm on then darling and could you get a tin of meat for Bobo please—please?

She listened to him move about in his room, slam cupboards, drawers, doors. The flat door. At the window she fingered the curtains, twitched them aside, and looked out, drew back, waited, looked again. A pigeon flew off the ledge, flew over into the square that was empty, except for a man who swept, pronged pieces of paper, rubbish. She faced the room, picked up the knitting, the cat, books, each held for a moment, pressed against herself. She switched on the radio, television, then off. In Leonard's room she looked at the heap of clothes, catalogues she picked up from the bed, flung back. Hell hell if only I knew—knew . . . She looked in the wardrobe mirror. Hell what can I do . . .

He nodded at the sweeper, who leaned against a bench. Cold today looks like rain. The man coughed, spat into the Keep Off The Grass patch. Got a light sir? Ah thanks might snow never can tell thanks very much. Mittened hands fumbled with the cigarette, touched his cap as Leonard swung away up the path. Across the grass, strips of brown, broken twigs. Grey branches struck the greyer sky. A faint sun became fainter. The high street a hum of traffic. He passed by. Scaffolding. Cranes. People carrying brief-cases. Bags. Umbrellas. He scanned quickly, then down. In a coffee bar he sat in a recess, hands arched round the cup. Looks like snow. The waitress said, bent over him. Still if it does never quite so cold. He looked up, but she had gone to manipulate the coffee machine. He took out a paperback, opened it, but looked through the dim lighting out of the window. A few white flecks, that could have been fluff, dust, fell, stopped, and fell again.

She lifted the tape recorder up, looked through the reels, and put one on, allowing it to spin silently, then she pressed down.

. . . of some exotic flower. Hovered over walls. Smell of . . . She pressed down again and moved the reel by hand.

. . . his mask. In the heat. The robes clinging. As a weekend. In a hotel room. Meals brought up. And not eating.

Avoiding

the issue

possibility. For the last time. Remembering only the first. Climb-ing the stairs. Knowing the receptionist looked. Two days. Nights. Spent in. Over. The bed. Heavy curtains . . . She switched off. Searched for a cigarette. What's the use—the use? She moved the reel round, and switched on.

. . . hurt me

there

here

anywhere. This way. If you like. Talk to me talk

Talk

to

me

Was it like this with

Never like this. Before. Like waves. The coming.

Slowly. Then the rush of it. Demanding more. But without asking.

Dual roles. Realised. Yes yes
Yes. Be a boy. If you like. Anything. Be
Just be.

The hot . . . She switched off. Carefully lowered the machine onto the floor. The cat looked up from the doorway. It doesn't mean a thing Bobo does it not anything. She picked him up, he licked her face, making her cheek more wet, but turned his head as she drew on the cigarette. She put him down, and called, fingers snapped. She made kissing sounds and went into the sitting-room. She opened the window and tried catching some snowflakes. In the street people quickened their pace. Lights came on. Traffic piled up, muffled, as snow fell heavily, faster. She banged the window down, and drew the curtains. In the dark she curled up on the sofa.

A group of girls entered, giggled, shook snow off their heads, coats, opened carrier bags. Rustle of paper, dresses. Heads bent over, close together. He stood up, paid the bill. Said it would snow didn't I thank you sir good day. He heaved against the glass door into the street. People pressed, bumped by. He stepped off the kerb. Matches sir buy some matches—matches . . . In the park he kept to the path uphill, breathing rapidly, his head down against the blizzard. The gates were being closed. He shouted out, and ran, slipping. His hat fell off. He cursed and picked it up. He shook the gates. Trudged through grass, and climbed over the railings. He crossed the road, turned the corner, paused, and jumped on a bus at the traffic lights.

She awoke with a start, switched on the light and looked at the clock. Lighting a cigarette, she stood at the window. Snow completely covered roofs, pavements wet only. She put the fire up, poured out a drink, and turned on the radio, which she hummed to, but stopped, sighed, and gulped the drink down, poured out another. She opened the journal, and began writing. Turned the radio down, listened to her own breathing, the cat's, sound of a piano played faintly from another flat. In the corridor she listened, opened the door as the lift gates were pushed aside, but quickly closed the door, as a couple, laughing, emerged. In the bedroom she pulled out some dresses, changed into one. Rearranged her hair, face, eyes. Sitting at the dressing-table, she stared into the mirror, until her eyes watered. She went into the other room. The tape recorder, reels, she pulled out, one by one. One separate from the rest, she put on. Leonard's voice, sharp, slowly came over. She turned the volume up, leaned over, eyes closed.

That I've been in a trance no doubt. Confronted by an existence I can no longer believe in. But who can say there's any definition in what has been? Three aspects yes yes that can be recognised. Now. The boy. Youth. Man. Each contradicting. How to come to terms? A compromise. In the dark my hand. Hands. That have touched known—no no no not that. Perhaps there is a fourth that has stood outside? Watched. A cheshire cat forming a grin inside a crack. She understood this. Perhaps not. An ambiguity certainly. The sensible husband. Practical. Desiring to do what is expected. Accepted. Adjusted to the role. A member of society. Composed. Controlled. Known for action alone. But back—back to the boy with the sad round eyes who watched from behind curtains others torturing cats dragonflies cut up worms and knocked old ladies' hats off. Whose laughter caught in the throat and fell asleep over books. Made princesses out of paper and set fire to them. The little soldier playing with real lives to create a bigger and better world where all things everybody would be equal. You believed in that. He did at least. The belief then was something concrete. Compartments were unknown. Only the whole a love affair yes not unlike. Constructing in a common knowledge a recognition that one instinctively went by. But a game nevertheless. Yes a game you—he watched played out against a background of subterfuge. Violence. Torture. Never witnessed. Only whispered about behind locked doors. Down with the Capitalists. But not the family the girl who cried when they took her parents away. Then was it then awareness shook the sleep-walker? The idealist. Tin soldiers grew life-size. Screamed. Shuddered. Between their legs a bridge that had no beginning no end. Contradict that if you can. I can. But this now brings no such certainty. What would it mean to her if ... She switched off. Listened to the hum of the recorder only.

Along the embankment, he walked, blinking away the snow. In the middle of the bridge he leaned over, watched its shadow, those of other bridges. He walked on. Into a pub and ordered a beer. Where people huddled, waited, given up waiting. Girls, with flushed faces, looked up, dismissed, turned their attention to a drink, cigarette, attempted to be intimate, less intimate. An old man leaned over a newspaper, jerked awake by his own snores. A woman talked to a dog that sniffed under her, legs, skirt. Someone suddenly shouted Oh God do you have to bring that up oh no the past is dead I tell you it's unnecessary to bring up the past really believe me so shut up for crissake will you he'll never know and as for her well what can she do—no no I tell you . . . He ordered another drink went over to a corner, surveyed the bar, mirrors reflected other mirrors, gave three images of himself, each dwindled, dimensions reduced by walls, tables, chairs. The door.

Outside the snow had stopped. A wind came up, blowing the snow, dust, pieces of paper against gutters, walls. He could not hear his footsteps, but looking back there were dark prints cutting the pavement up. He breathed into cupped hands, rubbed them, fistlike in gloves. Past statues with white wigs, heads. Birds silently winged over the river, dipped now and then against the wind. Somewhere an ambulance clanged. A train. He turned a corner, some children ran past, screamed, hurled snowballs, one hit the side of his face. They disappeared into a house. A woman's voice. A dog. A light in an upstairs window. A bottle of milk broken on a step, the milk frozen, whiter than the snow. The moon, a particle, appeared vanished, appeared again. He crossed a footbridge. A huddle of houses with identical façades, backyards, roofs. Roofs of cars ribboned with snow. Trees without branches, without snow, lined the road either side, elbows of bark. Yellow stained at the bottom where dogs had been. The trees ended where more houses, blocks of flats, closed up the area. His steps crunched, gradually a regular beat, as he approached the city centre. Here no sign of snow, except on a few cars making their way in. He entered a cinema without looking to see what was on. The place half empty. He sat in the next to last row, and closed his eyes.

She pressed the switch of the recorder, without looking, and leaned over the table, head against her arms.

Specified conditions bring a certain amount of satisfaction. There is no denying that. And yet—yet what pressure I might have put on her she surely asked for needed. I had no choice. She said there is no answer. It was understood. But all things considered it was a time when—how can I put it how describe how in recollection can one come to terms with what seems now to be looking back on yet another person another role? Even in that cell solitary confinement when time became meaningless even there I had the part to play out. A boy who saw himself the man with a cause not necessarily disillusioned oh no it never came to that. How could it? Never as sudden as that abides its time. There's never the point when one can say I am disillusioned now. But on looking back then one wonders at precisely what moment the illusion was shattered. On the other hand a feeling of being changed by others circumstances can be pointed out shaded in as mountainous country on a map. A change was admittedly known. But recognised only by myself. For others the pattern is set which they refuse to alter. Soon one believes that is oneself and the change settles into corners. Roused only in moments say by stimuli or objects. Smell. Sound. That remind. Then the image topples. But still no one notices. Least of all those living the most close to you. Least of all . . . Then there's subterfuge and one goes on automatically complying being doing. For that is the easiest way. Besides one soon forgets. Habits take over, the pain becomes an object looked at from a distance.

That she suffered there can be no doubt. I felt anxious. It was unpleasant. But there was pleasure. Not unshared. I . . .

Leonard's voice muffled, then high-pitched. Switching on the light, she looked down at the recorder, turned it off, and took up the spool. The tape broke as she tried to re-wind. Twisted as she straightened by unwinding further, until a twisting mass lay in her lap, curled about itself in her hands.

He looked up at the screen that showed a nudist colony. Large Nordic women bounced, laughed, and frolicked amongst trees, grass, with flowers in their long hair, holding bunches against breasts. The cinema dotted with men in brown, grey trilbies, damp coats folded on empty seats, or on knees. Someone wheezed behind. The usherettes giggled in front of the velvet-curtained doorway. When the lights came on torches were still automatically shone around. The snow had changed to sleet. He waved a taxi down. The seat was wet. He pulled the window up, sank back, blinking at the lights, traffic lights. Saying yes, or really, as the driver shouted remarks he did not hear. He jumped out, paid, and pushed through the revolving doors. The hall porter said something, but he saw only the man's mouth open, shut, behind the lift grille.

In the corridor he listened. The flat in darkness, except for the fire, its glow against the sitting-room wall. Ruth—Ruth where are you—Ruth? He opened the bedroom door, looked at the bed, around. Opened his own door. He knelt in front of the fire, rubbed his hands, face, and poured out a drink. Hearing a slight noise, he went into the corridor, pushed open the door slowly. Ruth what on earth are you doing in here? Something gone wrong with this blessed tape look at it sorry I seem to have made it worse some of it's broken. She held the spool of twisted thin brown towards him. Where have you been it's so late Leon I was rather worried? Went to the pictures caught in that blizzard sorry suppose I should have phoned. You've been drinking too phew phewey. She brushed by him, her nose wrinkled. What film did you see then? Oh not very good some western. You could have got a cab darling? Mmmmmm suppose so. He bent over the tape, the empty box. Why did you put this one on love? Thought it was hers sorry I didn't realise anyway half of it was damaged before I even tampered with the thing. He heard her bang about in the kitchen, talk to the cat, as he wound the tape back. Did you get Bobo's tin of meat darling? Oh God sorry forgot completely went out of my head. He shouted. Waited. Heard only the movements in the kitchen, sound of taps running. Fuck the bloody cat. Muttering he placed the spool in the box. In the doorway he watched her move about, methodically from one utensil to the next, her head bent over sink, stove. Veins stood out in her hands over the wooden spoon.

He poured a drink, switched the television on, and fell back on to the sofa. He made a kicking gesture at the cat walking towards him. He picked up a cushion. The cat sniffed his shoes. Shoooooooo go on shoooooo. Looking down he saw the open journal. He leaned over and began reading Ruth's large widely-spaced writing.

November 1st

I can feel nothing. Only think and wonder. Have I a responsibility to myself in as much as confronting him with my suspicions? No no it would prove pointless. But am I perhaps afraid of even confronting myself with the issue? If only we had a child. Does he wish this as much? Would it make me feel any different basically? The response is no longer there. This much I know. He is concerned only with achieving his own orgasm and I refuse absolutely to be exploited in that way. Has it ever been different when we first married? How difficult it is to remember past feelings. That I was passive too passive I realise he made me so. And in all that the wish to please satisfy what I thought he most wanted yet wanting myself something other something else. But exactly what? This morning he came to me, without looking, my body felt a slab of meat under his hands. There are days hours I long for something anything to happen. A certain tenderness. I am so tired. My body is heavy as heavy as thoughts and the cry is stillborn. I see him as from a cage. Then I think of them together. Yet there is nothing definite to go by. No substantial evidence as it were. At least everything here around us has substance gives security. A home we have built up together. But lately I have felt almost an intruder. Why? I look at myself and see what I might be like in five ten years time. Will things be any different from now? The toleration politeness that brings a basic relationship a certain smoothness in day to day living. But never laughter. Not that bursting laughter as a young girl even she had that, the slight gasp before the laughter is over, which I've never really experienced, never the awareness of being young or ever certain. Always holding back, things had to be relatively either black or white. I do regret not having lovers before marriage that is a fact. When we met he was a God, a brother I never had, perhaps a father too. His faults were endearing. I felt I understood. In awe of his idealism, intelligence, and above all secure in his respect for me. When did all that falter, what day, night did I feel this appalling separation, a certain loss of identity? The days they went off together, and I was left alone in the house, facing those broken statues, perhaps then, yes perhaps the realisation that here was someone who shared something with him I failed to find. Didn't I then immediately feel a kind of relief when she was dead, hadn't I almost wished this to happen? The time when we were on the bed together, her white neck, hadn't my fingers felt a strange tingling sensation, as though they were someone else's hands, a murderer's hands grafted? Then the dreams came, leaving a back-taste the rest of the day. But how can I be responsible, feel responsible for those? Her eyes at times as though she knew what I felt, was in fact the spinner of my dreams. I seemed to have no alternative. I somehow envied her life, that sense of freedom she so obviously had, when everything seemed possible. Yet at the same time there was pity, yes pity for what I saw in her eyes, and her desperate clinging to us. Which now I'm not so sure about. What did she want of us, need from him, myself? We shall probably never know. Now there are the nights of self-pity, wishing in a way he would leave. That I could go, but the effort. Effort. And we remain. I watch as a guest might. Waiting for his next move. An element of restraint is necessary, knowing there is at least a sense of power in such passiveness. And perhaps tomorrow.

Set the table darling. He heard her move back into the kitchen, amongst saucepans, plates. Cooking smells drifted into the room. He put the journal back under the cushion. Watched the television, sound turned down. A woman, hands pressed against herself, wide mouth, she jerked backwards, forwards.

Click of knife and fork. Her eyelids heavily blued. What shall we do tonight Ruth anything on the tele? Nothing much more vegetables darling? No thanks. Sure? Yes really thanks. There are plenty here have some more? No really I . . . She scooped the sprouts out, piled them onto his plate. Some wine love? Have we any? Half a bottle of Beaujolais. O.k. Warm enough? Fine. Ruth I've been thinking perhaps we ought to . . . Yes darling? She looked suddenly up, moved the candle aside so that she could see him. He looked at the television. You were saying? Maybe we could go away for Christmas? Abroad Leon? No no I mean to Grey House and not—well not have all that family business with father and everything here what do you think? I'd rather not go down there the place gets so cold and it takes days to warm up—besides . . . We've got to exorcise that place Ruth sometime. I wasn't thinking of that. She piled the plates together. It would be nice to have friends around so desolate down there in the winter Leon and—well there's not very much to do there nothing to see at least . . . But we never see anyone here love. Well we'll think about it heaps of time darling. Yes I guess so. He watched her move away from the table, about the room. Heard her in the kitchen. At the window he pulled back the curtain. The square opposite completely white. Streets had trenches of blackness. Wind blew some snow from trees, roofs. Tops of buses, cars, beds of whiteness.

He switched on the desk light, and opened a manuscript. Stared at the circle of light thrown on the paper. Coffee Leon—Leon do you want . . . Yes love yes. Turn the fire up darling it's freezing in here Leon did you hear? Yes all right all right. She watched him bend over the fire, straighten, his head twisting from side to side. She arranged some cushions on the floor and sank down. If you want to work I'll go in the other room? No no don't bother just reading. She wriggled amongst the cushions, brought her knees up. Ruth are you happy I mean . . . Happy darling what made you . . . Oh I don't know you seem somehow—well I don't quite know how to put it perhaps a little withdrawn lately are you worried about anything? No—nothing except possibly—oh it doesn't matter yes I'm happy of course I'm happy we're happy aren't we Leon I mean . . . He came to her, knelt, his head against her, he whispered. What? Just . . . What is it Leon? His head moved against her, up and down. Smell nice new perfume? Just soap or powder I guess. A new dress too? One of hers only one that fits. She touched his hair, cheeks. Her eyes closed. His hand touched the dress, traced the design, edged over, crept up her thighs, the flesh between stockings and suspender. Her hand came over his fingers that pinched, grasped, and climbed further up, then in. She looked down, trying to see his face, eyes. Eyes sunken. A wetness around his mouth. Veins swollen on his neck, forehead. His fingers pushed further in. Careful of the fire darling you'll get scorched. She pulled away. He fell sideways, laughing. What's so funny then? Arms outstretched, he lay on his back, still laughing, mouth closed, body heaved against her legs. She stood up, over him. He reached for her ankles, and looked up. Come—come to me? Not now not here Leon you look so ridicu-

126

lous like that for heaven's sake . . . She tried to turn, but his hands locked tighter round her ankles. Come Ruthey won't you—here? He pouted, tongue tipped his lips, drawn in, then out. One hand slid over her ankle. No—no Leon you know I don't like it with clothes on. Well take them off damn it. You're so crude sometimes ugh really how can you . . . Only normal Ruth for Christ sake vulnerable as any man would be. His hands released their hold. She remained standing, arms stiff at her sides, her mouth opened, as if about to say something. He folded up, head on his knees. Leon I'm sorry—sorry but . . . Oh doesn't matter. But really I am. She fumbled amongst his hair, but stepped back as he sat up, his eyes narrow, face flushed. What's happened to—happened to us Ruth lately what . . . Oh you you you . . . She spun round, and ran from the room. He heard her door bang, waited for the key to turn. He stretched out, his arms supported his head.

She buried her face in the pillow, legs drawn up under the eiderdown. She shook for some time, stopped, lay motionless, sniffing. She shook again. Turning over she stared into the darkness, at a light from the street. Tears glided down one side of her face, she did not brush away.

He knocked on the door. Ruth let's talk really we can't . . . He switched on the light. Put that out put it out please—please. He stumbled forward in the dark, heaved up onto the bed, touched her shoulder, and tried bringing her to him. She sprang back and curled up, shuddering against the wall. He searched for a cigarette, watched the red dot near, away from him, smoulder. Listen Ruth if you want . . . I don't want anything—just go—go on please—please leave me alone—alone. He tried to see her against the wall, clinging there. He sat up. Her hand came out, fists against him, in space, areas of darkness around him. He caught hold of her arms, and pulled her down under him. I hate you—hate hate hate . . . He pulled her dress up, slid the underwear apart, and went into her quickly, as she cried out, her arms above, hands clawed the wall. Her body sank into the bed, as he moved above her. Not like this oh God Leon not . . . He panted as he strove faster, deeper. You're hurting oh Christ it's hurting me don't—no Leon are you mad? She tried bringing her legs together. His knees pressed them further apart, his hands planted either side of her arms. She dug her nails in until her fingers were covered in his blood. Going to fuck you fuck you fuck you until . . . She screamed out as he went deeper in. She tore at his hair, face. He paused, turned his head away, began again, moved faster, until her bare thighs, belly smacked against him, and the springs of the bed creaked. Her body limp, head alone moved, twisted, came up, sank back, her mouth open, but no scream came. He withdrew, falling across her legs, his head over the bed. She tried manoeuvring herself from under him, but his body pinned her down. She flung her arms out, and pushed back, until he rolled over. She searched for the lamp switch. She shrank against the wall, looking at herself, at him, trousers hung round his ankles, shoes. He slid back into the middle of the bed, pulled the eiderdown over, until she saw only the hump of his body, and hair protruding. She stood up, pulled her dress down. Ruth I . . . Don't speak to me don't you dare . . . She went out, slamming the door.

He heard the bath water being run. Groaning, he pulled the eiderdown over his head, waited for his breathing to assume a normal rhythm, and closed his eyes.

She locked the door, and leaned against it, hands flat either side. Watched the water tumble into the bath, the steam engulf window, mirrors, walls. She stood on a stool and opened the window. She leaned out, head lifted to the snow, mouth open, where the flakes melted. Music, laughter drifted across from a room opposite. A couple kissed behind the curtain, their shadows merged, slid slowly apart, together.

He lit a cigarette, piled the pillows up, and rested against them. He picked up a mirror, grinned, a grin that grew into a frown, as his teeth gritted, jaw worked up and down. He rattled the handle. Ruth—Ruth look I . . . Sound of more water gushing, followed by splashing. He leaned against the door. Oh God God. He went into the sitting-room, picked up a book, books, which he opened, shut. The newspaper, page after page he turned over.

She lathered her hands with soap, and softly touched her breasts, lifted up, inspected, red marks she put more soap over. She slid down, until the water lapped her neck, chin. Sounds of music, laughter louder, someone screamed, turned into high pitched giggles. A scratching at the door made her lift her head. She climbed out of the bath, opened the door quietly, wide enough for the cat to squeeze by. She put a towel on the stool, beckoned to him, then picked him up, and put him there. She stepped back into the bath, shook the wet ends of her hair, hand held towards the cat, who put a paw out, then tentatively stepped onto the edge of the bath, and balanced his way along, until he was near her face. He sniffed at the water, whiskers, tail quivering. She brought her hand up, dripping with water. He jumped down, scratched the door, looked up at her, and mewed. She quickly climbed out, shivering, dried herself, and dressed. Rubbing the window she stared out, at the shadows opposite moving around each other. A thin moon hung between two chimneys, until clouds passed over. More chimneys in line, banked by snow, round black tops, or thin funnels in places, indistinguishable from the few trees. Multi-coloured lights from many windows. Yellow lights, from the streets, cast a heavy orange glow in the sky. Blue icicles made a formation of their own on the fire escape.

Hearing the door open, close, Ruth's steps in the corridor, he opened a book. Sound of the bedroom door, followed by the flat door. He leaned out of the window, saw her emerge. Watched her drive quickly up the street. The car slightly skidded on the corner. Pouring a large measure of whisky he went into the bathroom. Hearing the noise outside he looked across. A girl, in jeans, swayed in ballet positions at the top of the fire escape. A bunch of men laughing, stood at the window, held their glasses up. The girl looked down, giggled, and seeing Leonard, she shouted out. The men looked across, waved. Sounds of jazz floated out. The girl's mouth opened, but he could not hear anything, as she weaved her way round the black and white framework. She picked up a handful of snow and threw at the bathroom window, where it sprayed out, scattered in tiny blobs. He drew the curtains, but still heard the laughter, music, and saw his shadow spread over the curtains. Oh go to hell. He turned the taps on, and sat on the lavatory seat, breathed against the glass, gulped the whisky in small quick doses.

She drove fast along the main roads, turned off into a side street, and stopped. She climbed out and stepped carefully between lumps, tracks of blackened snow, up the steps, and rang a bell. A woman stood in the doorway. Sorry the doctor is not available. But it's urgent I must see him where is he? I'm afraid he's away can I do anything is there something—can I give you the name of a colleague perhaps? No—no doesn't matter I . . . Clutching handbag against herself, she ran down the steps. He'll be back next . . . She banged the car door, turned the ignition on, and spun the car round, drove slowly along narrow streets, empty except for parked cars, half embedded by snow. She stopped in front of a lighted window, and searched for a cigarette. Looking out she saw some old men, one woman, slumped in front of washing machines. The woman met Ruth's gaze, pulled at a scarf round her neck, until it covered half her face, she slumped back again. A car came by, slowed down, lights winking. She adjusted the mirror. The car pulled alongside. She glared ahead, aware of a man grinning, the headlights continued winking. And she heard the car hoot. Shifting round, she saw him wind his window down. She drove quickly, scattering snow, until she came to some traffic lights. The other car pulled up, close, and the man shouted. She made a face. He gestured. She saw then that he pointed at her erect indicator. The lights remained red for some time. The man continued laughing. Behind him a bull-dog stared gloomily out of the back window.

He rested his head against the bath, reached for the bottle of whisky, and poured, until the glass was nearly full. Balancing a book on the soap rack, he read, but the steam made his eyes run. He threw the book onto the floor. Looked in the mirror, rubbed his eyes, and raised the glass to his reflection. You fool—fool— bloody fool. He noticed his hand, the scratches, thin mauve tracks across the knuckles, which he touched, rubbed the dry blood away, but some more blood trickled across. He splashed with water, but still it flowed. He wrapped the flannel round, and stepped out. Drew the curtains apart. The room opposite lit by candles, three on the sill guttered. A few shadows mingled, separated behind the steady fall of snow that became sleet, snow again. Tall blocks of buildings, where lights went out, left gaps, holes, squares of dark- ness, edged with brittle white.

She drove into streets lined either side by tall warehouses. Neon signs swung, lettering broken up by snow. Along the embankment snow had drifted against trees, walls. The river, yellow, curled into purple mud. Boats like dead whales, upturned. Swans, folded in upon themselves, sheltered under a bridge. She drove slowly, now and then rubbed the windows. Patches of ice splintered under the wheels. A few large gulls circled high above the water, or perched in rows along the bridge parapet. A headless snowman, with branch arms, squat in the middle of some gardens. An old couple in a doorway ate fish and chips, faces averted as the car headlights swept across. A couple in evening dress waited outside a hotel for a cab to be called. Slush broke in shreds across the car windows. The road ahead clear, where snow had been swept into gutters. She drove up a cul-de-sac, reversed, and spun out into the main road. Spray from the river fell onto the pavements, pin-pointed dark crusts. She stopped and looked in the mirror, pressed a handkerchief under her eyes, powdered her face.

He closed his diary, opened it again, stared at the solitary black mark on the page, he doodled around. Small circles, and dots splattered to the edge from his pen. Hearing the door open, he closed the diary, picked up the newspaper, redirected the lamp, until the light shone on the headlines. He heard her steps in the corridor, saw her shadow against the wall, above the desk, waver there. He turned the newspaper over to the back page, aware now of her shadow falling away, her steps, a door closing. He stared at a painting above the fireplace. His hand curled over a catalogue cover of an orchid.

Undressing quickly, she slid into bed, nursed the cat under her arm. Gazed into the darkness. A speck of light shivered in the mirror.

He brought the lamp over to the table near the sofa. He reached for the newspaper, scanned the headlines, and paused over a small item at the bottom of the page

The unclothed body of an unidentified young woman, with stab wounds in back and abdomen, was found yesterday by a lake near the Sugarloaf mountain. A blood-stained angler's knife and hammer were also found.

June

This sudden heat-wave makes the nights long. Though a breeze usually comes off the sea just after the sun goes down, when trees, bushes stir in the garden, as if people are still there. Perhaps they are, for the beaches beyond the breakwater are crammed every day, and when it is dark, music from their transistors moves nearer, and laughter rises up below the garden. Sand in the mornings covered in foot-prints, and burnt grass near the dunes. L goes down occasionally, but by the time he reaches the steps, no one can be seen. Maybe they hide in caves, behind rocks. He stands at the top, never going down onto the beach, shines a torch around, and shouts who's there? The other night, while swimming, I saw the light from his torch. For a long time the light flashed across the shingle, breakwaters. Then darkness, but I could just make out he still stood on the top step. By the time I had come out, dressed, he had gone.

R moves slowly, heavily about, complaining of the heat. The cat sleeps in the terrace shade, or shadows of statues, all day long, only moves if a lizard scuttles from the grass. The pool hasn't been filled yet, so we continue going down, don our masks, move the statues around. At times the place takes on the appearance of a temple, or an open tomb, with flowers scattered about. Even with nothing on under a thin dress, my body becomes sticky, and an awareness of every limb, unlike the separation felt during winter.

Yesterday afternoon we went onto the beach, taking food and

drink. R fell asleep. I gave myself up to the sun. Dreaming dreams only such dazed warmth can bring. L poked a stick amongst rocks, pools, or his fingers groped under stones, pulled out shells, cleaved open, only to find them empty. He manoeuvred a large crab onto the stick, and shouted to us. Look look what I've found. R sat up, startled, wiped the corners of her eyes. Oh put it back. She said. Poor thing—let it live. But laughing, he brought the crab over, it fell off the stick, and lay so still we thought it dead. But as L bent to pick it up, the crab danced sideways into his shadow, clumsily seeking shelter, turned, and began digging into the sand, as we watched. L touched it with the stick, and it made for a rock, but our shadows made it change course. R screamed as it came towards her. There was one claw missing. L, still laughing, jumped on the crab and moved his foot several times, before looking down at the broken remains of shell, claws, greenish fluid. R had reached the cliff and fanned herself with a straw hat. L picked up the crab's remains, and did a crazy dance towards her, arms, hands made tentacle gestures. I stood at the edge of the sea, my legs planted either side of a castle he had made. When I turned, I could not see them. Only heard their laughter. R's voice loud at first, then low, coming from a cave. Outside, on a sandy ledge, the crab's remains, and long thin fish bones, gulls' feathers, scattered around the hat, straw faded, whiter than the cliffs. I swam out to the end of the breakwater, climbed up, and lay down, drowsed by the distant sounds of people, sea. I must have fallen asleep, though I could not be certain, except the tide had reached a much higher mark on the breakwater than I had expected. They were nowhere to be seen, and thinking they might still be in the cave I went over. So dark inside it took some time before my eyes grew accustomed to the change. I called out, but only my own echoes answered. Under my feet many carcasses of fish, shells. Heard strange sucking noises from rocks around. I turned back, on hands and knees. The dim light from outside expanded gradually like the palpable flesh from the under-side of some monster.

In the evening we made plans for climbing the Sugarloaf the next day. Though R was not very enthusiastic. In such heat she said it would be heavy going. We decided to take the car so far, and leave it somewhere near. We marked a route on the map. I longed so much to be close to that lake, which I had seen only from the far distance, looking so unreal, at times not like water at all, but a strip of steel, or just a field of blue flowers. We arranged to start early in the morning. Just after midnight I heard a slight patter on the roof, at first I thought it might be mice, or the cat, but gradually the patter broke into a steady fall of rain, like nails hammering against the house, which continued all today. R seemed relieved, played, sang at the piano, brought out the cards. While L shut himself up in the summerhouse, where he also took his meals. I stayed for a little while, watching him spray the orchids. Small colourless buds he brought down, parted the leaves to show me, like someone with a child, pulling back a hood, stroking away hair from the eyes. Bending close, he one side, myself peering down, making appropriate remarks, attempting to see what he saw, felt. And outside the rain slashed the paths, statues. Steam rose from the weeks of dry ground.

This afternoon the rain stopped. Everything dripped above a brilliant green undergrowth, as if a painter, obsessed with only that colour, had swept a series of canvasses, in every possible light and shade, then varnished haphazardly, spilling over the edges.

L and I went for a walk. Clouds had lifted from the mountains, which seemed larger than ever before, and nearer. The sea stretched out, hardly moved, though waves broke against small islands, like shoals of fish turning over and over. The sand was very damp, even several layers underneath. Though drier amongst the dunes, where we rested. A slight wind came up, blew the sand across our legs, rippled against the grass. Mountains changed from blue to purple, but green reflected in the water. L seemed preoccupied, even when I spoke, attempted to speak, he did not listen, and if he glanced in my direction, when offering a cigarette, his eyes were glazed. Even a fly on his arm did not disturb his thoughts. A circle of mosquitoes whirred continually above. A small boy sat on the breakwater, legs swinging, he stared over at us. A group piled out of a car. They danced past him. L, as if shaken suddenly awake, brushed the sand away from his clothes, hair, and helped me up. I waved to the boy, but he did not respond, only pushed his large hat further over his eyes, and made a kicking gesture with legs, and arms.

Early this evening I saw the fires along the beach, and went down, mingled with several groups. Guitars were played. Girls danced with each other, or on their own. Couples disappeared behind breakwaters, reappeared, no longer held hands, separated when approaching the fires. Stars seemed nearer, so near, to be almost touchable. Some fireworks were set off, becoming indistinguishable from stars that fell. Mountains were pyramids, or Egyptian mummies, rising out behind the sea. When I arrived back, the house was in darkness. I felt more than a mere trespasser as I opened the door, made for my room. But what is there to take, other than what they have set out as decoys to distract from the main objective. After all I have become the victim now, and from that there is no turning back.

Thursday

This afternoon L went to his room, saying he was not to be disturbed, as he had a lot of work to get through. I took some tea in. Admittedly the desk overflowed with paper, books, but the sofa, cushions were also in a state of confusion. He looked like a child caught stealing, who persists in keeping up the pretence. When I went into R's room, she asked if he was working hard. Games that would be difficult not to join in. And in such secrets, however small, I share with either of them, there is a feeling of— how can I say—a sense of closeness. A conspiracy in a way, when each knows that only I can play at traitor if I choose.

Friday

We went for a picnic in the car, as the weather looked bright before setting out. But by mid-day drizzle began. And everything enveloped in thick sweeping mists, making trees at times appear human. We returned, silent, as though some unspoken row had taken place, and none of us prepared to give in. It became smoky, dark, damp in the car. As a train passed I envied those who were going somewhere, or coming back. Held in that timeless area between one point and the next. Yet perhaps those faces behind carriage windows wished they were us in these surroundings of a perpetual changing landscape. But nothing really varies inside the house. Even moods between them can be regulated, recognised, stemmed from an action, non-action, each might consciously or unconsciously perform. But how easy it is to deceive them by my own expressions. And I cannot deny a certain amount of pleasure in adopting an outward aspect, contrary to what my real feelings are. So that when the storm broke out tonight, and people entered the garden, with torches, fireworks. Instead of joining in, I remained by the window, my hands folded in my lap. But laughter bubbled up inside me, especially when I noticed, in the flashes of lightning, L's face behind the summerhouse glass, and heard R's frightened cries. All was over far too soon. Though for the first time the gardens look alive. Even the statues seem human, so much so that at times I wonder if perhaps they are, maybe a few people remained. By torchlight, the imprint of flowers looked like tracings, or claw marks on the paths. A balloon in the empty swimming pool drifted between broken statues, like some planet out of orbit.

Midsummer's Eve

We decided to mime, L and myself, while R took the cine camera down. But we had not been miming for long, before the riot broke out. I noticed them first, half a dozen or so faces over the edge of the pool. Then things were thrown down. And suddenly three of the statues moved towards R. Screaming she dropped the camera, and ran along the platform. L for a moment stood still, then realising he jumped forward. R continued screaming. For a time I couldn't make out anything, hardly see, as earth, metal pieces, broken bits of bronze fell around. When finally I could see, L lay flat on the ground. He was being beaten up by three men, whose faces, arms, legs were whitewashed. How patiently they must have waited, motionless, for us to come down, arranged themselves amongst the statues, not daring even to breathe. They looked like clowns giving vent to years of repressed feelings, as they punched, and kicked L. By the time I reached him, they had fled, yelling, waved at the top of the steps, before disappearing. R crouched against the wall, in a corner. I helped L up, his face one mass of blood, clothes torn. He clutched a glove, gasping I'll get them I'll get them for this they won't get away this time. The garden was in wild disorder. They had broken into the summer-house, and torn orchids from the pots, that lay between scattered broken pieces of statues.

Apart from a few bruises, and a black eye, L had not been badly hurt. He insisted on wearing bandages round his head. He went to the police station later in the evening, handed over the glove, and made a lengthy statement. He returned, convinced they were mad there too, he felt they hadn't really believed him, kept giving each other knowing looks, winks. As if I'd go to all the trouble of making such things up. He said, while sticking parts of sculpture together. You've got the cockerel's head back to front. R pointed out. It's bronzed eyes now stare from the terrace at the house.

It has taken us several days to clear the garden, pool up. And this afternoon we remained indoors, though the sun has been shining all day. Having very little to do, we decided to mime. R joined in for a time, but soon became bored, or exhausted by L's elaborate directions before beginning. This now is a prison—you can't go more than three paces to the left or right and only six front and back. I noticed the sweat roll from under L's mask, as he pressed against space. Writhed on the carpet. Clawed the air around. At times he seemed to forget we were supposed to be miming only, and he'd gasp, groan loudly, as he crawled within a space the chairs created. He knelt for some time, twisted his hands, fingers, close to his masked face, until R, laughing, asked what he was supposed to be doing. I'm contemplating hanging myself. He whispered. He stood on a chair, and mimed an extraordinary grotesque scene, the longest I've ever seen him perform. I clapped enthusiastically when thinking it over. But touching his neck he stretched up from the chair. Ducked his head, until at last he jumped from the chair, his head rolling, tongue lolled out. He collapsed on the floor, laughing, and went on laughing, shaking from head to foot. They say one gets an erection that way. He shouted at R. But she had gone to prepare tea. And did you? I asked. He shook his head, sat up, turned the mask over and over, held against his face, peered through the slits and said No—well not exactly—as you can see there's no mandrake sprouting at your feet . . .

Monday

The weekend has gone so quickly, that it is difficult for me to recollect everything in detail. So many people, all at once, suddenly descended. A party evolved, that lasted pretty well throughout the night. Though she retired early, I have a somewhat hazy memory of seeing R in her nightdress at the top of the stairs. She looked down at me, at a man who kissed my feet. Again I thought I saw her in the garden, floating between statues, like some ghost longing to take on a human form. But there were many women in long dresses, white, pale blue, pink, and in that semi–darkness it was difficult to see who might or might not be there. The same person who had kissed my feet, I later saw embrace a headless statue, pour drink over heavy stone breasts, while a girl, hung upon his arm, and tried pulling him away. Later I remember looking for L, but could not find him. Once I thought I saw him behind a statue kissing a woman, but as I passed I could see it wasn't. Strange to recapitulate the feelings then, fluctuating. Especially when in the morning we were surrounded by the debris, people bundled under coats on the terrace, and a record spinning on in silence. Still later that day, a stillness, only broken by R piano playing. And L complained of a hangover, saying never again. All seems now a dream, attempts at piecing together, and other dreams only are remembered.

Several evenings now I've taken the boat out, rowed towards the mountains. Such an overall quietness that I feel an intruder, and often just let the boat drift with the tide. Perhaps the idea evolved on just such an evening—but to write down would almost be like performing the action itself. Yes it is best to let it nurture. There is time yet. Besides to climb the mountain in the summer would be taxing. And come the autumn, there are the neap tides. How easy for a body to drift out, caught up in a current, and never be discovered, or for anyone ever to be certain. The time is not right at the moment. This summer must be lived through. Somehow. With them. There are admittedly moments when I wonder why I have remained as long as this. Was there hope at the beginning? How difficult it is to judge even one's own actions. There never appears to be only the one reason.

Yesterday evening when rowing past the breakwater, I recognised several of the men who had beaten up L. They played some game with knives on the sand, and beckoned me over. At the same time I saw L sitting on the top of the steps, it could have been no one else, the way his head jerked, twisted, from side to side, I could see even from that distance. I rowed quickly back. He came to meet me, helped to tow the boat in. I wanted to say something then, anything, everything. But he suddenly said I'll race you back, and leaping forward, he ran, kicking up shingle, sand, that I closed my eyes against.

Nights are filled with odd sounds. Crickets spinning away like bicycle wheels. Gulls mewing, sometimes all night. So near. Near. At times I think it might be R crying. But I cannot be sure. A simple recognition is all that's needed. Maybe I will make them realise this later. But later. When the nights draw in.

Last night, after dinner on the terrace, I tried persuading L to go down for a swim. He shook his head, though hardly aware I spoke. Half way across the garden I looked back and saw R at her window. L bent over his glass. But by the time I reached the cliff edge, I saw only the faint light of his cigarette, and the light went out in R's room. The moon full, made the sand like ice, the waves broke as snow against rocks. In the distance fishing boats bobbed up and down. Mountains part of the sky. Emerging from the sea, I stepped on a dead gull, wings stretched out, but looking as if capable of suddenly flying off. I picked it up, carried over to a sandy part between some rocks, and put it there. Wings spanned the rocks either side. There was no sign of blood. So white. Smooth. When I arrived back, L seemed glad to see me and poured out a drink. His neck, chest, white, where the shirt opened. But his hands quite brown.

This morning we all went onto the beach. R found the dead gull which by then was covered with flies. Feathers, blood scattered about. L picked it up by a wing, and threw into the sea, but the tide washed it back onto the beach, so he carried it further out. Behind the breakwater the beach was packed. I went across, and bought some ice creams. A ball thrown in my direction, I threw back. When I returned, L was busy pushing sand over the burnt remains of bonfires near the dunes. He spent part of the day discussing plans for keeping trespassers away.

After lunch a wind rose. Even in the shelter of the cliffs, our clothes, paper flapped. We decided to go for a drive to the other side of the mountains, where we had never been. Like entering another country. No wind, or if there was, the mountains held it off. We drove along many roads, which only ended in tracks leading to marsh land. Dead trees floated, some like enormous heads reared from the green mass. It was difficult to realise just the other side, the land altered into something tangible. We went up, through the tunnel pass, and stopped, looking at the valleys stretched out before us. The lake so small, that it might have been a mirror flashing in the sun.

Again tonight I went down on my own for a swim. The wind had dropped, but the water was colder than the night before. I sheltered afterwards in the cave. And smoked. Remembered other caves. Caves of our own making, that could alter to our own alteration.

For days now the rain has not ceased. We decided to go back to town. But no sooner had we returned than the heatwave began again. People sit outside pubs, in gardens, on balconies, in parks. Their faces seem more expansive, as convalescents, aware of their bodies, their surroundings, in a heightened way. But this hardly lasted, and soon everyone starts to grumble.

The cat began having tapeworms, and R bought various powders, he refused to take, and when forced, is promptly sick. Yesterday L found his bed one mass of little lumps of vomit. Furious, he picked up the cat, and threw him across the room. They had a row, that wasn't really patched up, before L was called abroad to meet a publisher.

R suddenly like a child, whose parents are out of the house, grew restless. We went for long shopping expeditions. Hairdressers. Films. Theatre. Like playing with dolls again, she said, as we tried on dresses in her room. But she grew more uneasy when no letter, not even a card, arrived from L. Today she remained in bed, asking me to stay with her. The room was stuffy, but she refused to have the window open, or the curtains drawn back, and lay, half naked under the sheet. I brushed out her hair. Ran a bath for her. While she chattered continually. A certain intimacy sprang up between us, that somehow never exists when L is around. So much so that I found myself wishing he would remain away longer. As if R plays a role when he is with us. Except I wonder if it is not a certain role she plays with me, when we are on our own.

L arrived back a day earlier than expected. He brought some white robes for our mime plays. He tried on over his clothes. R declared hers was too small. As the heatwave continues I wear mine, and nothing else, giving a freedom of movement around the flat, that strangely enough also gives me a sense of power. You look like a priestess—a sort of goddess. He said. You might wear something underneath you know it's rather transparent. R said. As she put on one of her new dresses, sprayed herself with eau-de-cologne. Oh it's unbearable this heat if only it would change. She kept saying. And at night under a single sheet, I remembered other nights spent in the hotel, the curtains drawn. The smell of our bodies, drink, tobacco. Pretending to be asleep, aware he looked down at me, and distant sounds of others in other rooms. Emerging on the third day, when everything, everyone seemed so distant. We were invisible. Contained in our bodies, that had crossed borders never before realised. Attempting to hold onto the smell of each other, knowing only too soon, soon it would evaporate, something which would be impossible to recall. But the sense of touch, fantasies re-explored. Pretend I'm tied to the bed. And his tongue whipped over, across, under. Have you tried it with three? Have you? Be three now. And incest? Whip me with your hair. Let me come between your breasts. In your mouth. Ear. Hollow in your back. Hair on his chest burnt with a cigarette. Brushing my hair in half darkness, a slant of light in the mirror, half dressed, conscious he looked, but when turning round, his eyes closed. What are you thinking? Of you. Thinking now? That this could last like this. When will you fuck me next? I'll fuck you any time you want. Out of the window. In a boat. An aeroplane. Unnecessary to move. But we moved over the edge of the bed. He standing up, holding onto himself, bending. Visions of forests in rain. A sweep of rocking vegetation. Clinging to wet rocks, the sound of fish leaping, or was it just our bodies? And one stem reaching up from undergrowth.

We walked in parks, but hardly any space to sit down. We went in a boat on the river. Then they decided to go back to the country, before autumn settled in. Even now the leaves are changing. At night I lie awake thinking. Thinking. Planning.

This morning I got up early and went for a walk. Crossed over the breakwater, and several others. Behind one a party of cripples lay. A few men without arms were in the water. Some sat in pools. Behind them, rising out from mist I could just see the peak of the Sugarloaf, as though floating on its own. If I closed my eyes I could see the lake, that flat piece of stillness, glinting in sun, as though a particle of the moon had fallen. But I knew it could be touched, and would not be fragmented by my touch.

Today the first signs of a sharpness in the air. The mist rises up from the ground lying in thin frost. The boat is ready, as planned. And all that's necessary now is a note. I know nothing will change.

Dear readers,

As well as relying on bookshop sales, And Other Stories relies on subscriptions from people like you for many of our books, whose stories other publishers often consider too risky to take on.

Our subscribers don't just make the books physically happen. They also help us approach booksellers, because we can demonstrate that our books already have readers and fans. And they give us the security to publish in line with our values, which are collaborative, imaginative and 'shamelessly literary'.

All of our subscribers:

- receive a first-edition copy of each of the books they subscribe to
- are thanked by name at the end of our subscriber-supported books
- receive little extras from us by way of thank you, for example: postcards created by our authors

BECOME A SUBSCRIBER, OR GIVE A SUBSCRIPTION TO A FRIEND

Visit andotherstories.org/subscriptions to help make our books happen. You can subscribe to books we're in the process of making. To purchase books we have already published, we urge you to support your local or favourite bookshop and order directly from them – the often unsung heroes of publishing.

OTHER WAYS TO GET INVOLVED

If you'd like to know about upcoming events and reading groups (our foreign-language reading groups help us choose books to publish, for example) you can:

- join our mailing list at: andotherstories.org
- follow us on Twitter: @andothertweets
- join us on Facebook: facebook.com/AndOtherStoriesBooks
- admire our books on Instagram: @andotherpics
- follow our blog: andotherstories.org/ampersand